HarperCollins®, ☙®, and HarperEntertainment™ are trademarks of
HarperCollins Publishers.

Iron Man: The Junior Novel
Printed in the United States of America. No part of this book may be used or
reproduced in any manner whatsoever without written permission except in
the case of brief quotations embodied in critical articles and reviews.
For information address HarperCollins Children's Books, a division of
HarperCollins Publishers, 1350 Avenue of the Americas,
New York, NY 10019.
www.harpercollinschildrens.com

Library of Congress catalog card number: 2007938651
ISBN 978-0-06-082197-5

❖

First Edition

STARK INDUSTRIES

IRON MAN
The Junior Novel

Written by Stephen Sullivan
Based on the Screenplay by Mark Fergus & Hawk Ostby
and Art Marcum & Matt Holloway
Based on the Marvel Comic

HarperEntertainment
An Imprint of HarperCollinsPublishers

CHAPTER

1

Lieutenant Colonel James Rhodes, Tony Stark's best friend, stood at the podium and narrated as a film about Tony's life played on a huge conference screen. The film showed Tony's privileged childhood, his first-class schooling, and his amazing ability to design and build machines.

"Since inheriting Stark Industries from his father," Rhodey said, "Tony has worked on innovative high-tech projects. He designed the experimental ARK Reactor and has created many of the new smart weapons systems that help keep all of us safe. Today, Tony Stark's ingenuity continues to protect freedom and American interests around the world."

As Rhodes wrapped up his speech, an inspiring shot of the American flag, waving dramatically, filled the screen. The show ended and the lights came up.

"Ladies and gentlemen," Rhodey said, "this year's Apogee Award winner . . . Mr. Tony Stark."

The crowd in the auditorium broke into thunderous applause. A spotlight moved across the stage and landed on . . . an empty chair. The applause quickly faded into surprised murmurings.

Rhodey gritted his teeth as Obadiah Stane, Stark Industries's second-in-command, strode out onto the stage and took the podium.

"Thank you," Stane said. "I, uh, I'm not Tony Stark. But if I were, I'd tell you how honored I am and . . . what a joy it is to receive this award." He took a deep breath and forced a grin. "The best thing about Tony is also the worst thing—he's always working."

But Tony was *not* working. In a nearby Las Vegas casino he sat at a gaming table, betting enormous amounts of money. He paused and threw the dice, turning up another winner. The crowd around the table cheered.

Just then, Tony spotted Rhodey striding toward him across the casino floor.

"Rhodey!" Tony exclaimed. "What are *you* doing here? They roped you into this awards thing, too?"

Rhodey scowled at him. "Yeah. They said you'd be deeply honored if I presented the award."

Tony stood up and straightened his tie. "Okay," he said. "Let's do it."

Rhodey plopped the Apogee Award down on the gaming table. Tony stared at it, surprised.

"That was quick," Tony said. "I thought there'd be more of a ceremony or something." He picked up the dice, shook them, and rolled—but they came up losers. The crowd around the table sighed and glared at Rhodey, as though he had brought Tony bad luck.

"My chaperone has just arrived," Tony announced to the crowd. "I must now take my leave—along with a generous helping of the casino's money."

He collected a huge stack of chips from the table and headed for the door. As Tony passed, people gawked and took pictures of him with their cell phones.

"A lot of people would kill to have their name on that award," Rhodey said angrily.

"It belongs to my old man," Tony replied. "They should have given it to him."

Rhodey glared at his friend. "What's wrong with you? A thousand people came here tonight to honor you, and you didn't even show up. This award means something, Tony, it's bigger than you. It's—"

"Hold that thought," Tony said, meandering over to a roulette wheel. He set down his mountain of chips.

"Put it all on black," he told the operator.

The uniformed woman spun the wheel. The ball circled several times, bouncing off numerous numbers and colors before finally ending on . . . red.

Rhodey gawked. "You just blew three million dollars!"

"Yeah," Tony replied. "I don't know which was more exciting: winning it, or the fact that I don't care that I just lost it."

Rhodey was furious. "We've got a long day ahead of us tomorrow," he said. "Can we get out of here now?"

"One more stop," Tony insisted, and strode toward the restroom. Once inside, he splashed water on his face.

"This is no joke," Rhodey said, following him. You're going into a war zone tomorrow just to show off some crazy equipment. We should be doing that here in Nevada."

Tony sighed. "This system has to be demonstrated under true field conditions."

Just then, the door to the restroom swung open and an attractive redhead in her late twenties walked in. Rhodey recognized Virginia "Pepper" Potts, Tony's executive assistant. She wasn't the kind of person who let a MEN'S ROOM sign get in the way of doing her job.

"Tony, it's the president," she said. She tossed him a cell phone, turned, and walked back out.

Tony put the phone to his ear. "Jim," he said, "how're the trout running?" On his way out of the restroom, Tony dumped his Apogee statue in the attendant's tip basket.

Pepper joined Tony and Rhodey as they headed for the casino's front door. "Tony, you're leaving the country for a week," she said. "I just need five minutes of your time."

"Okay," Tony said. "Shoot."

She tapped the screen of her PDA. "The board meeting is on the eleventh. Should I tell them you'll be there?"

Before Tony could answer, an attractive young woman holding a digital voice recorder pushed her way through the crowd. "Mr. Stark!" she called. "Christine Everhart, journalist. Can I ask you a few questions?"

"Can I ask you a few back?" Tony replied, slowing down to talk.

"You've been described as the da Vinci of our times," Ms. Everhart said. "What do you say to that?"

"Ridiculous," Tony said. "I don't paint."

"And what do you have to say about your other nickname: the Merchant of Death?"

Tony rubbed his chin. "That's not bad," he began flippantly, but an icy stare from the reporter stopped him.

"Look," he said, "it's an imperfect world. I assure

you, the day that weapons are no longer needed to keep the peace, I'll start manufacturing bricks and beams to make hospitals."

"Rehearse that line much, Mr. Stark?" Ms. Everhart asked.

"Every night in front of the mirror. But call me Tony."

She frowned. "I'm sorry, *Tony*, I was hoping for a serious answer."

"Here's serious," he said. "My old man had a philosophy: Peace means having a bigger stick than the other guy."

"Good line," she replied, "coming from the guy selling the sticks."

The remark stung. "My father helped defeat Hitler," Tony said, his teeth gritted. "A lot of people—including your magazine bosses—might call that being a hero."

"Others might call it war profiteering."

Tony chuckled. "Tell me, Christine Everhart," he said, "how do you plan to report on the millions of people we've saved by advancing medical technology? Or the millions more we've kept from starving with our intelli-crops? All those breakthroughs were spawned by our military projects."

Without waiting for a reply, he turned and left the casino.

CHAPTER

Tony Stark's mansion home stood atop a tall bluff on the edge of the Pacific Ocean. The house was a sprawling, ultramodern building—all glass and shining steel. It sat precariously on the edge of a cliff, giving its owner a commanding view of the surf far below.

Tony wasn't admiring the view, though. As usual, he was working in the huge laboratory-garage beneath the mansion. This morning, his project was tuning up one of the cars in his collection, an old '32 Ford. He looked up as Pepper entered the workshop.

"Boss," she said, "you still owe me five minutes—"

"Just five?" he asked, cutting in. "We really should spend more quality time together." He smiled at her, but she merely sighed.

"Focus," she said. "I need to leave on time today."

"Why the rush?" he asked. "Do you have plans tonight?"

"The MIT commencement," she said, forging on. "Yes or no?"

"Maybe. Tell me your plans."

She punched the touch pad on her PDA. "I'll tell them yes. Do you want to buy the Jackson Pollock painting? The owner has another buyer in the wings."

Tony frowned. "What does it look like?"

"It's a minor work from his later spring period," she replied. "It's ludicrously overpriced, and—"

"Buy it."

"Hang on," she said, tapping the phone head-set that was perched in her ear. "Nope," she said to the person on the other end. "He left an hour ago. Okay." She clicked off the receiver. "That was Rhodey again."

Tony gazed into her eyes. "You have plans tonight, don't you?" he said.

Pepper lifted her perfect nose just slightly. "I'm allowed to have plans on my birthday."

"It's your birthday again?" Tony said.

"Yep," she replied. "Funny—same day as last year."

"Well, get yourself something nice from me," he said.

"I already did," Pepper said, smiling indulgently. "Thank you, Mr. Stark."

"You're welcome, Ms. Potts."

James Rhodes paced the tarmac. "Where is he?" he grumbled. Behind him, Tony's private jet sat waiting.

Just then, a sports car roared up, a Rolls-Royce limousine right beside it. Tony's chauffeur, Hogan, popped open the Rolls's trunk and pulled out Tony's overnight suitcase. Tony hopped out of the car.

He waved at Rhodey and headed directly toward the jet. "Sorry," he said. "Car trouble."

Rhodey followed him to the plane, fuming. "I was standing out there for three hours!"

Tony shrugged. "I had car trouble."

"What? You couldn't pick *one* car so you had to take two?"

"If you're in such a hurry," Tony said, "let's get going." He walked up the stairs into a jet bearing the company slogan: STARK INDUSTRIES—TOMORROW TODAY.

Hogan stowed Tony's overnight bag aboard the plane and went back to the Rolls. Rhodey wondered who would pick up the sports car. "The problems of the rich," he muttered to himself as he hurried up the gangway.

The flight attendant shut the cabin door as Tony and Rhodey settled in to the jet's plush, leather seats.

"You want a drink?" Tony asked.

Rhodey shook his head. "Let's just get this show in the air."

After dinner, Rhodey and Tony got into another argument. "You just don't get it," Rhodey said, annoyed. "I don't work for the military because they paid for my education; it's a responsibility to our country."

Tony regarded his friend coolly. "All I said was, with your smarts and your engineering background, you could write your own ticket in the private sector." He flashed a smile. Rhodey folded his arms across his chest.

"And working as a civilian," Tony continued, "you wouldn't have to wear that military straitjacket."

"Straitjacket?" Rhodey blared. "This uniform means something! It means a chance to make a difference. You don't respect that because you're not listening to a word I'm saying."

"I *am* listening," Tony insisted. "But I've heard you give this speech before. First you reflect on the new American century, then you embark on a history of World War Two and the Tuskegee Airmen, and then . . ."

Rhodey unbuckled himself and got up, looking to escape the billionaire's harangue. "You know, the heck with you," Rhodey said. "I'm not talking to you anymore." He stormed off toward the cockpit.

"Sure," Tony called after him, "go hang out with the pilot. You'll get along well. He's got a personality just like yours."

Rhodey strode to the cockpit and yanked open the door. But there was no one there; the pilot and copilot's seats sat empty. The jet was being flown by one of Stark's sophisticated computer systems.

Rhodey scowled, walked back to the rear of the plane, and plopped down into his seat.

Tony chuckled.

"Very funny," Rhodey said.

"I thought so," Tony replied.

They spent the rest of the flight in silence.

The next morning, they touched down in Bagram Air Force Base in Afghanistan. Once there, a convoy of Humvees took them from the base to a fortified test site in the desert.

As Rhodey settled in among the generals and VIPs, Tony went to work. He walked up and down the makeshift stage, boasting the virtues of Stark

Industries's latest equipment.

"The age-old question," Tony said, "is whether it's better to be feared or respected. I say, is it too much to ask for both?"

His eyes gleamed as he walked over to a Jericho missile perched atop a mobile launcher.

"With that in mind," Tony continued, "I present the crown jewel of Stark Industries's Freedom Line of armaments. This is the first missile to incorporate my proprietary Repulsor Technology—or RT, as we like to call it—a breakthrough in energy control and guidance."

He pressed a button on a remote, and the missile streaked into the air. The rocket arced gracefully toward a nearby rocky mountain peak.

"Fire off one of these babies," Tony said, "and I guarantee the enemy is not going to leave their caves. For your consideration . . . the power of Jericho."

He pointed as the Jericho missile divided from a single weapon into a swarm of mini-missiles. The missiles smashed into the nearby peak. With a deafening roar, the mountain exploded into a shower of debris.

Dust washed over Tony and the generals. Tony continued smiling, unfazed by the sudden blast. The generals and Afghan officials nodded and muttered among themselves, impressed.

"Gentlemen," Tony said, "Stark Industries operators are standing by to take your orders." He walked off the stage to where Rhodey stood waiting.

"I think that went well," Tony whispered to his friend.

"What are you going to do next?" Rhodey asked.

"Call the home office," Tony replied. "They'll want to know how the sales pitch went." He pulled out a satellite video phone and punched in a number. A moment later, Obadiah Stane's weary face appeared on the screen.

"What are you doing up so late, Obadiah?" Tony asked.

"Sleeping," Stane replied. "How did it go?"

Stark grinned. "I think we've got an early Christmas coming."

"Sounds good," Stane replied blearily. "I'm hanging up now. Bye."

Tony passed the phone to Rhodey, and then walked over to a row of soldiers waiting by the group's Humvees. "All right," Tony said, "who wants to ride with me?" Reading the name tag of a young soldier nearby, he asked, "Jimmy?"

Jimmy's young face lit up. "Me?" The two soldiers with him—Ramirez and Pratt, according to their name tags—nodded as well. Tony and the three soldiers piled into the vehicle. Rhodey was about to get in as well, but Tony stopped him.

"Sorry, Rhodey," he said. "No room for my 'conscience' in here. See you back at the base."

As Rhodey headed for another vehicle, Tony slammed the door shut. Ramirez cranked up the stereo, and their Humvee roared off into the desert.

CHAPTER

Tony watched as the bleak landscape of Afghanistan rushed past the Humvee's window. The vehicle was cramped, sweaty, and hot—a far cry from the air-conditioned luxury Tony had known all his life. He adjusted the collar of his expensive suit and glanced at the soldiers riding with him. None of them seemed bothered by the heat or the bumpy road. Buried under their gear, all three soldiers looked alike to Tony.

"Oh, I get it," Tony said after a time. "You guys aren't allowed to talk. Is that it?"

"No," Jimmy replied. "We're allowed to talk."

The soldier whose name tag read "Ramirez" flashed Tony a beautiful smile. "I think these boys are just intimidated."

Tony nearly jumped. "You're a woman!" he blurted.

The other soldiers chuckled.

Tony's face reddened as he straightened up in his seat. "I would apologize for not realizing, but isn't that what we're fighting here for? The right of all people to be equal?" He smiled back at her, but Ramirez merely shook her head.

"Mr. Stark, sir?" the recruit named Pratt asked. "Can I take a picture with you?"

Tony looked at him seriously. "Are you aware that Native Americans believe photographs steal a little piece of your soul?" For a moment, Pratt looked worried. Then Tony added, "Not to worry, mine's long gone. Fire away."

Grinning, Pratt crowded next to Tony as Jimmy framed them in a digital camera. Tony unbuckled his seat belt and put his arm around Pratt's shoulder.

"Say cheese!" Jimmy said enthusiastically.

Just then, a huge explosion rocked the truck. Tony watched through the windshield as an enormous ball of fire knocked the Humvee ahead of them off the dirt road.

Tony slammed into the side of the Humvee. His gaze fell on the right sideview mirror just as the Humvee behind them blew up.

Trapped between two burning vehicles, Tony's Humvee skidded to a stop. The sound of gunfire rattled the Humvee's windows. At that moment,

Tony regretted ever going Afghanistan to promote his new weapons systems.

"Stay here!" Pratt commanded. He, Ramirez, and Jimmy piled out of the Humvee, ready to fight. As they left, another explosion filled the air with dust.

Tony peered out the window, trying to see what was happening. A face appeared on the other side of the glass: Lieutenant Colonel James Rhodes.

"Get down, Tony!" Rhodey commanded. "Get—"

A nearby explosion cut him off. Rhodey whirled, firing his machine gun through the dust. He ran into the billowing cloud, trying to secure the Humvee's position.

As Tony ducked down, yet another explosion rocked the vehicle, shattering the window above his head. A shower of glass rained down on Tony's two-hundred-dollar haircut. The attackers, whoever they were, seemed to be getting closer with each shot. Tony knew he was doomed if he stayed in the Humvee. So he scrambled across the seat and out the far door.

Tony stumbled across the rugged landscape, looking for cover. Smoke stung his eyes and the sound of gunfire echoed in his head. The whole convoy had ground to a halt. They were trapped.

Something landed nearby with a soft thud—an unexploded rocket-propelled grenade. Tony gaped at the info stenciled on the side of the explosive:

USM 11676—STARK MUNITIONS

The enemy was shooting at him with weapons made by *his company.* Tony turned and ran. *Please let it be a dud!* he thought. *Please let it be—*

A blaze of blinding white light surrounded him as the grenade went off. The blast hurled Tony through the air and he landed hard on the ground. The air rushed out of his lungs, and the world around him faded away.

When Tony came to, he found himself tied to a chair in a dark cave. Ragged, makeshift bandages covered his body. Every part of him hurt—especially his chest. It was all he could do to stay conscious.

Two scruffy guards, armed with machine guns, stood nearby. On the other side of the cave, a video camera focused on a tall man who seemed to be the leader of these people. Tony realized the men must be insurgents—the rebel fighters who had attacked his convoy. The tall man read a prepared statement for the camera in a language Tony didn't understand. Next to the man stood a line of armed, hooded men holding up a banner showing ten interlocking rings—a sign Tony had seen before on the news. It was the symbol of a well-known insurgent faction.

The leader finished reading and thrust a huge, sharp knife into the air. The others cried their approval. The cameraman turned the camera toward Tony. The leader stepped forward, his knife gleaming in the semidarkness. Thankfully, Tony passed out.

When Tony opened his eyes again, he was in some kind of emergency room—though it didn't look like a very good one. He was strapped to a bed and connected to numerous wires and tubes. Everything around him, even the medical equipment, looked dirty and ill-repaired. An aging man in a dirty doctor's smock stood by a nearby sink, shaving. He didn't notice that Tony had woken up.

Feeling thirsty, Tony reached for a pitcher of water on a nearby table, but it remained beyond his grasp; the tubes and wires connecting him to the medical machines wouldn't let him stretch that far. He grabbed hold of the wires and pulled, trying to rip them out. Somehow, he didn't have the strength. His chest ached terribly.

The doctor noticed his efforts. "I wouldn't do that if I were you," he said in slightly accented English. His dark eyes strayed meaningfully down the wires to a nearby car battery. A chill rushed down Tony's spine. Who were these people? What had they done to him?

He put his hand on his bandaged chest and suddenly realized he was in the hands of the enemy. He'd been taken prisoner—and they'd done something to his heart.

CHAPTER

4

Tony faded in and out of consciousness for a long time. When he could finally focus again, he was in a cave. The doctor stood a dozen yards away, stirring a bubbling pot over a small gas-fired furnace. It looked like he was working on an experiment. Flickering fluorescent lights dangled overhead. A closed metal door seemed to be the room's sole exit. Dirt, grease, and blood stained the doctor's yellowed smock. He had a tanned, wrinkled face, gray hair, and thick glasses. He glanced over as Tony stirred.

Tony looked at his chest and gasped; a bulky metal chest piece protruded from beneath his fresh bandages.

"What have you done to me?" he asked.

The doctor stopped stirring the pot. "My name is Yinsen. I saved your life. I only removed what I had to." He picked up a jar from a nearby shelf and tossed it to Tony. "Here. Catch."

Tony, who was no longer strapped down, caught the jar and winced. His chest felt very, very strange. "What is this?" he asked. The jar was filled with tiny pieces of barbed metal.

"A souvenir," Yinsen replied. "I took those barbs out of your chest, but I couldn't get all of them."

Tony looked at his wound and suddenly felt sick.

"Don't worry, though," Yinsen said. "I anchored a magnetic suspension system to your chest plate. It's holding the shrapnel in place . . . at least for now."

Tony looked at the nearby car battery, connected to the wires on his chest, and shuddered. Then he noticed a security camera perched high on the cave wall.

Yinsen nodded. "That's right; we're our own TV show, you and I. Smile."

Somehow, Tony didn't feel like smiling.

"We've met once before," Yinsen continued, stirring the pot, "at a technical conference in Bern, Switzerland."

"I don't remember," Tony said.

"You wouldn't," Yinsen replied. "For all the partying you did, you gave a surprisingly good talk on integrated circuits."

Just then, a metal slat in the middle of the door slid back, revealing two menacing eyes.

Yinsen stopped stirring. "Stand up!" he hissed at Tony. "Do as I do. Now!"

Tony tried to stand, but couldn't manage it. Yinsen dropped his spoon and helped Tony up.

"Listen to me," he whispered. "Whatever they ask you, refuse. You understand? You *must* refuse!"

Before Tony could ask why, the door swung open and a tall, powerful-looking man entered, flanked by two armed henchmen.

The man began speaking in Arabic and Yinsen translated. "Abu Bakar says, 'Welcome, Tony Stark, the greatest mass murderer in the history of America. It is a great honor.'"

Bakar held out a surveillance photo showing an image of the Jericho missile test. He continued talking.

"You will build for him the Jericho missile you were demonstrating," Yinsen translated.

Tony took a deep breath. His chest ached dully. "I . . . refuse," he said.

Yinsen leaped forward and slapped Tony across the face. Yinsen's eyes burned with anger. "You refuse?" he raged. "You will do everything this man says! He is the great Abu Bakar! You are alive only because of his generosity. You are nothing. *Nothing!* He offers you his hospitality, and you answer only with insolence? He will not be refused. Obey him or you will die!"

Tony's cheek stung. He took a step back.

Abu Bakar chuckled. Then, with a nod of satisfaction to Yinsen, he turned and left. The guards went with him. As the door slammed behind them, Yinsen let out a sigh of relief.

"Perfect," he said. "You did very well, Stark. Good."

Tony sat back down on his cot, confused.

Yinsen smiled. "I think they're starting to trust me." He returned to his kettle. Tony realized suddenly that Yinsen wasn't working on an experiment—he was cooking.

Tony's stomach growled hungrily. "What's next?" he asked.

Yinsen shrugged. "We've reached the end of my plan," he said. "From now on, we improvise."

Tony walked blindly for long minutes until one of Bakar's henchmen yanked a smelly hood off of Tony's head. Blinking against the sudden light, Tony found himself in a valley surrounded by tall mountains. The day's brightness stung his eyes, and it took him a moment to process all he was seeing.

Skids piled with weapons surrounded him. All of the munitions—some dating back twenty years—bore the Stark Industries logo.

"Quite a collection, isn't it?" Yinsen said as he watched Tony's shocked reaction.

Tony shook his head in disbelief. "How did they get all this?"

Abu Bakar spoke.

"As you can see," Yinsen translated, "Abu Bakar has everything you will need to build the Jericho. He says you should make a list of materials. You will start work right away."

Tony looked around the valley, his eyes settling on a man nearby. He recognized the man from military briefings; he was a warlord called Raza—a leader of the Ten Rings rebels.

"When you are done," Yinsen said, still translating, "Bakar and his friends will set you free."

"No, he won't," Tony said.

"No," Yinsen agreed quietly. "He won't."

General Gabriel walked alongside Rhodey as he picked through the charred wreckage from the ambush. "What a mess," the general said, shaking his head.

"Something's not right," Rhodey said.

"It looks like a standard hit-and-run to me," the general replied.

"Sir, I'm telling you, this was a snatch-and-grab," Rhodey insisted. "As soon as they got what they wanted, they melted away—and what they wanted was Tony Stark."

"Intel's on it," Gabriel said. "If Stark is out there, we'll get him back."

Rhodey took a deep breath. "General, with your permission, I'd like to stay and head up the search."

"Negative," Gabriel replied. "Right now, the best way for you to serve your country is to get back to the United States and handle the firestorm of publicity."

"Tony Stark is the Department of Defense's number one intellectual asset," Rhodey countered. "I can be of more value in the field, getting him back."

"Duly noted," the general replied. "But we need you back home." He turned and walked toward his staff car. "Lieutenant Colonel," he called back, "it is not lost on me that you and Stark are lifelong friends, but—in this instance—there's nothing I can do."

A few days later Tony, wrapped in an army surplus blanket, sat next to Yinsen's portable furnace. Yinsen was cooking again. Tony wondered if he ever used the furnace for anything else.

"I'm sure your people are looking for you, Stark," Yinsen said, "but they will never find you—not in time."

"In time for what?" Tony asked.

"In time to save your life," Yinsen replied. "That car battery attached to your chest plate is running out of power. Bakar won't turn on the permanent generator until you start to work for him."

"And if the battery goes, I die," Tony said.

Yinsen nodded. "You'd have minutes to live. Hours, if you were lucky. You don't like what you saw in that valley, do you?" Yinsen said. "I didn't like it either when Stark-manufactured weapons destroyed my village. What you just saw is your legacy—your life's work in the hands of these murderers."

Tony said nothing.

"Is that how you want to go out?" Yinsen asked. "Sitting silently in a cave? Is this the last act of defiance of the great Tony Stark? Or are you going to try to do something about it?"

Tony rubbed his head. "Why should I do anything?" he asked. "They're either going to kill me now, or the barbed shrapnel will kill me in a week."

Yinsen looked into his eyes. "Then this is a very important week for you."

CHAPTER

Abu Bakar turned on the lab's new, portable generator.

"Okay," Tony said, trying to think of a way out of the mess he'd gotten himself into, "here's what I need to build your weapons. . . ."

Yinsen cleared his throat and began translating Tony's list for Bakar.

"S-category missiles," Tony said. "Lot 7043. The S-30 explosive tritonal, and a dozen of the S-76. Mortars: M-Category, numbers one, four, eight, twenty, and sixty. M-229s—I need eleven of these. Mines: the pre-nineties AP fours and AP sixteens."

Bakar relayed the orders and his men hurried off to fill Tony's requests.

Tony made an arc with his hands. "I need this

area free of clutter," he said, "with good light. I want the equipment at twelve o'clock to the door, to avoid logjams. I need welding gear—acetylene or propane—helmets, soldering setup with goggles, and smelting cups. Two full sets of precision tools. . . ."

Bakar seemed annoyed by the long list.

"Finally," Tony said, "I want three pairs of white tube socks, a toothbrush, protein powder, spices, sugar, five pounds of tea, playing cards, and . . . a washing machine and dryer."

Bakar pushed his face right up to Tony's and spoke in Arabic.

"A washing machine?" Yinsen translated. "Do you think he's a fool?"

Tony stared into the insurgent's eyes. "I must have *everything*," he said. "Great man will make a big boom for the powerful Abu Bakar. Big boom will kill Bakar's enemies."

Yinsen translated and, slowly, Abu Bakar nodded and smiled.

The next day, Tony and Yinsen began salvaging the pieces they needed from the aging weapons Bakar's men had brought.

"You know that Bakar removed all the explosives from these before he gave them to us," Yinsen whispered.

"I know," Tony replied. "They're crazy, not stupid." He carefully removed a tiny strip of palladium metal from one of the missiles.

"This is what we're looking for," he said, holding the strip up. "I need eleven of these."

It took hours for the two of them to collect the strips they needed.

Tony wiped his brow. "I assume that furnace of yours is good for more than just cooking?"

Yinsen nodded. "How do you think I worked the metal for your chest plate?"

"Good. Now heat the palladium to 1825 degrees Kelvin."

Yinsen put the strips in the furnace. "How will I know when it reaches that temperature?"

"The palladium will melt," Tony replied. As Yinsen heated the metal, Tony wrapped a copper coil around a glass ring he'd removed from another missile. They had a lot to do, and not much time.

"Careful . . . ," Tony said as Yinsen brought him the melted palladium.

"Relax," Yinsen replied. "I've always had steady hands. It's why you're still alive."

They poured the palladium into the ring and waited until it cooled.

Yinsen looked puzzled. "What are you building?" he asked.

"A better mousetrap," Tony replied.

They kept working around the clock, neither man resting or sleeping. Finally, Yinsen took a break to shave and wash up.

"What are you shaving for?" Tony asked, annoyed. "We're almost done."

Yinsen carefully scraped the straight razor over his whiskered face. "Look like an animal, and soon you'll start behaving like one."

Tony frowned and kept working. He finished connecting the last pieces of the device and threw the lab generator switch. The lights in the cave dimmed and the palm-sized device glowed atop the workbench.

"That doesn't look like a Jericho missile," Yinsen observed.

"That's because it's a miniature ARK Reactor," Tony said. "It powers the Repulsor Technology that should suspend the shrapnel in my chest and keep it from reaching my heart."

Yinsen nodded, understanding. "So you won't need the car battery anymore."

"Yeah," Tony said. "And this power source will last a bit longer than a week."

Yinsen leaned close, studying the device. "It's pretty small," he said. "What can it generate?"

"Three gigajoules per second."

Yinsen's mouth dropped open. "That could

power your chest plate for fifty lifetimes!"

A sly grin crept over Tony's face. "Or something really big for fifteen minutes." He held Yinsen's eyes for a moment and then said, "Let's install it in my chest."

Yinsen glanced at the security monitor that was tucked into a corner of the cave ceiling. "They'll be watching."

"Then I'll be counting on those famously steady hands to work quickly . . . and in secret," Tony said.

Weeks later, Tony bent over some salvaged sheet metal, cutting, welding, and bending it into shape. The laboratory was strewn with parts that might, for all his captors knew, be assembled into a high-tech missile.

Yinsen had taken to doing some odd things while not working. At the moment, he seemed to be assembling some kind of game.

"What are you doing?" Tony asked.

Yinsen looked up. "Tell me what you're doing, and I'll tell you what I'm doing."

"It looks like you're making a backgammon board."

"I'm impressed," Yinsen said. "How about we play, and if I win, you tell me what you're really making."

"Two things," Tony said. "One, I don't know

what you're talking about. Two, I was the backgammon champ at MIT four years running."

"Interesting," Yinsen replied. "I was the champion at Cambridge—the one in England."

Tony leaned away from his work and rolled his eyes. "Please don't use the words 'interesting' and 'Cambridge' in the same sentence. Is Cambridge still a school?"

"It's a university. You probably haven't heard about it since Americans can't get in."

Tony shot him a look. "Unless they're teaching."

Just at that moment, the door to the lab flew open and Abu Bakar stormed in, followed by four of Raza's guards. The guards took up positions on either side of the room and pointed their guns at Tony and Yinsen. After the room was secure, Raza entered. Everything about him screamed "danger." He seemed unpredictable and deadly.

"Relax," Raza told the guards. He walked to the workbench and looked at the missile schematics Tony had drawn on salvaged pieces of paper.

"The bow and arrow was once the pinnacle of weapons technology," Raza mused. "It allowed Genghis Khan to rule from the Pacific to the Ukraine."

The warlord fixed his cold eyes upon Tony. "Today, whoever has the latest Stark weapons rules these lands. Soon, it will be my turn."

Seeming to sense something was amiss, he turned to Yinsen and spoke in Urdu.

Yinsen shook his head and replied, adding in English, "We're working. The missile is very complex. That's why we're taking so long. We're working very hard. Ask Stark if you don't believe me."

Raza glanced at Stark. Tony remained stoic.

At a nod from the warlord, the guards seized Yinsen and forced him to his knees. Raza stepped forward and slapped Yinsen, continuing to ask questions in Urdu.

Tony winced with every blow. The warlord was trying to beat the truth out of Yinsen. Just as Tony was about to fight back, the guards let go of Yinsen, and he collapsed to the floor.

"Stark is building your bomb!" Yinsen gasped. "I swear! You'll get what you want!"

Raza scowled at Yinsen and Tony. "Time is running out," he said. He turned and left the room. The others followed, locking the door as they left. Tony helped Yinsen to his feet.

"That's twice I've saved your life," Yinsen said. "Now, are you going to tell me what you're really building?"

Tony looked at Yinsen. Even after all they'd been through together, could he trust him? Tony decided he could. Being careful to avoid the gaze of the surveillance camera, he showed Yinsen the real plans for the project.

Yinsen's weathered face broke into a smile.

Over the following days, the two of them worked feverishly: soldering circuits, connecting electronics, hammering metal—always carefully concealing their purpose from the watchful eyes of the warlord and his guards.

"My people have a tale about a prince," Yinsen said as he worked the salvaged metal. "The king hated the prince, so he banished him to the underworld and jailed him there."

Sweat poured from Tony's body as he beat the metal into shape. "Tell me," he said.

"The king made the prince work the iron pits. Year after year, the prince mined the heavy ore, becoming so strong he could crush pieces of it together in his bare hands."

Tony wiped the soot from his face.

"Too late the king realized his mistake," Yinsen continued. "He took his finest sword and went to kill the prince. But when he struck, the sword broke in half. The prince himself had become as strong as iron."

Tony lifted a glowing iron mask from the furnace. The mask was crude, but it would definitely suit his purpose.

"What next, young prince?" Yinsen asked.

CHAPTER

Several weeks later, Pepper strode down the executive hallway at Stark Industries headquarters. Rhodey and Obadiah Stane stood ahead of her, engrossed in conversation. Both men looked upset, and Pepper knew why.

As she approached, Stane sighed and went into his office. Rhodey headed for the door, but Pepper intercepted him.

"So that's *it*?" she asked angrily. "You're giving up the search for Tony? Everyone's pulling the plug and moving on?"

Rhodey shook his head. "There's nothing left we can do. It's been weeks. If there was any indication that Tony was still alive—"

"Spare me," Pepper hissed. "I read the official email. I thought that maybe, as Tony's best friend, you'd have something different to say."

She turned on her heel and stormed into her office. Rhodey followed.

"Pepper—" he began. But before Rhodey could say another word, Pepper stopped him.

"If anyone could figure out how to beat the odds, it's Tony," she said. "If it was *you* over there, he'd be finding a way to get you back."

Rhodey moved close to Pepper, so that no one else could possibly hear him. "That's just what I *am* going to do," he said. "You can't tell anyone this, but I'm going back to Afghanistan—and I'm not coming home without him."

Pepper smiled. "Maybe you *are* Tony's best friend after all."

Lieutenant Colonel James Rhodes stood on the tarmac at Edwards Air Force Base, a duffle bag slung over his shoulder, waiting in a line of soldiers. Everyone in line saluted as General Gabriel pulled up in a golf cart.

"What do you think you're doing, Rhodes?" Gabriel barked.

"Going back there, sir," Rhodey replied.

The general shook his head. "Listen, son, it's been three months without a single indication that Stark is still alive. We can't keep risking assets—least of all you."

"Are you blocking my transfer, sir?" Rhodey asked.

General Gabriel gazed down the line of soldiers. "Any one of these guys would kill for your career, Rhodes," he said. "Are you telling me you're willing to sacrifice that to fly desert patrol halfway around the world?"

"I am, sir."

The general took a deep breath. "Then I have only one thing to say. Godspeed." He saluted.

Rhodey saluted back and climbed aboard the plane.

Tony finished adjusting the carefully positioned tinsel strips and the laser in the tiny boxlike device. He checked the camera in the corner, remaining out of sight as he worked. It had been difficult to disguise what he and Yinsen had been doing over the past weeks. This device would make it easier.

He peered through the hole in the front of the box. Inside was a perfect holographic projection of the lab, with the furnace flickering in the darkness.

Taking a deep breath, Tony crept beneath the surveillance camera, and pushed the box into position. To anyone watching, it would appear as though the lab was quiet, and both men were sleeping. They could only use the box for brief periods before its batteries needed recharging, but hopefully that would buy them enough time to do their secret work.

Tony pulled back his shirt, revealing the glowing Repulsor-Technology "heart" keeping him alive. He plugged a long wire into the chest plate and then attached a sensor on the end of the wire to his leg.

Yinsen positioned an electronic contraption that looked like a piece of hinged metal on a table-top nearby. He nodded and held his breath.

Tony flexed his leg. The glow of his chest plate, which was powering the device, dimmed slightly. The beat-up laptop attached to the device whirred, making the necessary control calculations.

The contraption on the table jumped, moving in the exact same way that Tony's leg had.

The two men looked at each other, triumphant.

Tony unplugged the device. "We're ready," he said. "A week of assembly and we're a go."

"Then perhaps it's time we settle another matter," Yinsen said.

Tony nodded and switched off the hologram projector.

Soon, he and Yinsen sat across the lab table from each other, playing backgammon while they ate.

Yinsen studied the board. "Ah, anchoring with thirteen-seven. You know, I have never met anyone who understands the nuances of this game like you, Stark."

"Right back at ya," Tony replied. "Yinsen, you've never told me where you're from."

Yinsen paused and moved his piece on the board. "I come from a small village not far from here," he said. "It was a good place . . . before these men ruined it."

"Do you have a family?"

"When I get out of here, I am going to see them again," Yinsen said. "Do you have family, Stark?"

"No."

Yinsen leaned back in his chair. "You're a man who has everything . . . and nothing."

Without warning, the viewing slat on the door opened, and Abu Bakar stormed in.

Yinsen pointed to a pile of neatly folded laundry, stacked near the washer and dryer that Tony had demanded as part of his working bargain, and said something in Urdu. Bakar grabbed his laundry, lifted it to his nose, sniffed, and smiled. He walked back to the door, pausing only long enough to sneer at the two men.

"Yeah, yeah," Tony said. "Enjoy your laundry." He and Yinsen turned back to their game.

Just then, Raza entered the room.

Raza lunged forward and punched Bakar in the

face. Bakar collapsed to the floor. Raza's guards came in and dragged Bakar out.

The warlord turned to Tony and Yinsen. "You have until tomorrow to assemble my missile—or you will suffer the same fate."

The warlord stared at the men for a long moment before he turned and exited. His guards closed the door behind him.

Neither Tony nor Yinsen spoke.

Then, suddenly, a cold smirk broke over Tony's face. "Well," he said, "that's one less guy we have to fight on our way out."

In Raza's control room, Khalid watched the monitor nervously. He'd seen what they'd done to Bakar, and he didn't want the same thing to happen to him.

On the screen, Yinsen worked furiously, cutting and welding. Sparks flew, at times obscuring the camera's view.

Raza entered the control room and glanced at the monitor. "Khalid," he said, "where is Stark?"

With a shock, Khalid realized that he hadn't seen Stark in some time. It was too early in the day for Tony to be sleeping. He tapped the monitor, as though that might somehow make Stark appear.

"Go find out," Raza growled.

Khalid rushed down the hall to the laboratory door and opened the viewing slat. Inside, Yinsen continued to work furiously. Stark was still nowhere in sight.

"Yinsen!" Khalid called. "Yinsen!"

But Yinsen didn't turn away from his work. Khalid's stomach lurched. Yinsen and Stark were up to something.

He fumbled with the keys, unlocked the door, and pulled it open.

As he did, an explosion rocked the hallway, blasting him back against the wall and knocking him unconscious.

Yinsen waved the smoke from the explosion away from his face. "That won't buy us much time," he said. "How are we doing?"

Tony studied the laptop control screen. The program bars were all maxed out.

"It's frozen!" he said. "The systems aren't talking to each other. Reset!"

Yinsen came to his side and looked. "No," he said. "They're moving—very slowly. We can't start again. We don't have time."

He pressed a control button on the lab's winch and lowered a huge, metal chest piece over Tony. Stark connected the armor's electronics as Yinsen used a power drill to seal him inside the suit.

Yinsen looked at the laptop. The bars continued moving very slowly. They could hear the guards outside.

"Get to your cover," Tony said, his voice echoing inside the metal suit. "Remember the checkpoints—make sure each one is clear before you follow me out."

"Sorry, Stark," Yinsen said. "They're coming and you're not ready to go yet. If I can just buy you a few minutes more . . ."

He turned and ran into the hallway, scooping up Khalid's weapon from the floor.

"Yinsen!" Tony called.

But it was too late. Yinsen ran into the hall, firing the machine gun, trying to keep the guards back.

"Yinsen!" Tony called again, but his friend didn't reply.

Tony looked at the program bars on the laptop, but they were still moving so slowly. Gunfire sounded in the corridor outside. He could hear men running toward the lab.

Now! He needed the programs to finish now!

Suddenly, power surged and the lights dimmed into darkness. Two guards rushed in, firing. Tony grabbed them with his armored hands and threw them aside. As he approached the door, he saw his reflection in the shaving mirror on the wall.

He was huge and bulky, like a walking tank. Crude, gray metal armor covered him from head to toe. The Repulsor-Technology ARK generator glowed softly in his chest plate.

He'd become like the prince in Yinsen's story— a man of iron.

As more guards raced into the hall beyond the lab, Iron Man crashed through the doorway.

CHAPTER 7

The guards in the hall fired their weapons. Iron Man surged forward, bullets ricocheting off his armor. His heavy feet pounded the floor, shaking dust from the tunnel ceiling.

Seeing that their bullets had no effect, the guards jumped on him, trying to drag him down. Iron Man tossed them aside: The powerful motors in his armor gave him great strength.

Through the faceplate of his visor, Tony saw—in the distance—light from the cave exit. He lumbered forward, knocking guards out of his way as he went. An insurgent jumped out of a side passage and fired at point-blank range. Iron Man's armor dented, but the bullet still bounced off. He batted the guard aside.

More guards appeared before him, and then

more still. Iron Man kept moving, picking up speed like a freight train. He plowed through the enemy, knocking them down like tenpins.

The constant hail of bullets was taking its toll, though. Tony felt the armor bending and weakening around him. Smoke rose from the suit's seams. Tony knew he needed to escape before the suit sustained more damage.

The tunnel opened up into a wide cavern, the main chamber of the complex. The exit beckoned on the other side, but between it and Tony stood a dozen of Raza's men. Yinsen lay crumpled on the ground near the exit, wounded.

Raza's men raised their weapons.

"Look out!" Yinsen cried.

Iron Man turned just in time. A rocket-propelled grenade whizzed past his shoulder and exploded against the wall behind him. The wall crumbled and clouds of dust and smoke filled the room.

Through the debris, Tony spotted Raza, holding the grenade launcher. The warlord smiled and calmly loaded another grenade. Iron Man whirled on Raza, activating the flamethrowers that were built into his armor. Flames shot out of his hands toward the warlord.

Raza screamed and ducked for cover, dropping the launcher. The weapon exploded as the flames hit it, and part of the tunnel collapsed around the warlord. Iron Man spun toward the exit and turned on the flamethrowers again. The guards blocking his way ran. In moments, only Tony and Yinsen remained in the chamber.

Iron Man thumped across the room and knelt awkwardly at his friend's side. Yinsen's wounds looked very bad.

"Why did you run out before we were ready?" Tony asked. "We could have made it—both of us. You could have seen your family again."

A weak smile cracked Yinsen's blackened face. "I'm going to see them again," he said. "They're waiting for me."

In an instant, Tony understood. Yinsen's family was already dead—and Yinsen would soon join them.

"Don't . . ." Tony began, but it was too late.

Yinsen's eyes closed, and he slumped to the floor.

Rage filled Tony as he rose to his feet. He screamed as he barreled down the tunnel and out the side of the mountain. As he emerged, the warlord's men kept firing, denting and tearing tiny pieces off Tony's armor.

Iron Man surged forward, heading for the ammunition dump. A maze of boxes, all packed to the brim with weaponry, filled the valley.

Iron Man thundered into the maze. The boxes towered around him—enough armaments to start a war. Tony's eyes stung as he saw the Stark Industries logo emblazoned on the weapon crates. He fired his flamethrowers, and the boxes exploded in flames.

Raza's men followed him in, shooting as they came. The bullets ripped into Iron Man's armor. One caught on a seam and slammed into Tony's shoulder, knocking him off his feet.

His armor moved slowly and the joints ground together as Iron Man rose. Weapon crates burned all around now, but Raza's men didn't seem to care; they wanted to bring Iron Man down for good.

Tony knew the suit couldn't take much more—pieces were already beginning to rattle loose.

He fired one last flame at the weapon crates, then opened a metal flap on the armor's right arm. He flipped the switch inside and a screeching jet-enginelike whir filled the maze. The remaining guards covered their ears and fled.

Tony blasted off, soaring into the air like a rocket. As he went, the ammo dump began to explode—first one crate, then another, and then another, until the whole thing went up in flames.

Sweating, battered, and bruised, Tony concentrated on flying. He shot through the sky like a human cannonball. The desert streaked past below him, the scenery becoming a blur of speed and motion.

He thought he saw something in the distance. Were they helicopters? Were Raza's men still chasing him?

Then, suddenly, his jet boots gave out.

Tony plunged toward the sand, trying desperately to control his flight, but it was no use. He hit hard, spinning and rolling as he plowed into the ground. Pieces of his armor shredded off as he went. Finally, he skidded to a halt. The Iron Man armor was heavy against his skin.

He looked at his chest plate. The ARK generator glowed very faintly. If he used much more of its energy, his heart would stop. Tony cut the power to the suit and slowly, painfully, dragged himself out of the shredded armor. Behind him, explosions from the ammo dump echoed like distant thunder.

He had to keep moving. Raza's men would be after him.

He staggered to his feet, leaving the shredded armor behind, and limped across the desert, away from Raza's camp. His shoulder ached where the bullet had hit him. He clutched the wound, trying to stop the bleeding.

Don't pass out, he told himself. *Don't pass out.*

He kept walking for as long as he could. But

soon he couldn't go any farther. He hadn't eaten, or slept, or had any water since leaving the camp. "Should have thought of bringing supplies," he told himself as the sun beat down on him.

He closed his eyes to try to block out the glare, but his eyelids didn't want to open again. Something pounded in his ears.

High above him he spotted a helicopter. The sound was very close, almost on top of him. He tried to run, but his legs wouldn't move.

He couldn't believe it. He'd come all this way, only to be recaptured! His strength gave out, and he slumped blindly toward the sand. A pair of strong arms caught him. "Seems like saving your butt is getting to be a full-time job," a familiar voice said.

Tony's eyes flickered open and he looked up. It was Rhodey.

"About time you got here," Tony muttered, through parched lips.

CHAPTER

Days later, the Air Force C-17 transport carrying Tony back to the United States touched down on the runway at Edwards Air Force Base. Tony, who was seated in a wheelchair, waited beside Rhodey as the plane's rear ramp descended.

As Rhodey wheeled his friend off the plane, Tony spotted Pepper standing near the terminal. "Help me out of this thing," Tony said. He struggled to his feet and Rhodey steadied him.

"I got you, pal," Rhodey said.

Together they walked to where Pepper waited, standing beside Tony's limousine.

"Thank you," Pepper said, nodding appreciatively at Rhodey.

Rhodey smiled.

Tony took a deep breath as Pepper turned toward him. He didn't need to see the sympathy on her face to know how bad he looked. He was *not* the same man he'd been before Raza captured him—he would never be.

"Your eyes are red," Tony said to her. "A few tears for your long-lost boss?"

"Tears of joy," she replied. "I hate job hunting."

Pepper helped Tony into the limo and then climbed in herself.

"Where to, Mr. Stark?" Tony's chauffeur asked, hopping behind the wheel.

"We're due at the hospital," Pepper said.

"No," Tony replied. "To the office. I've been held captive for three months. I want to hold a press conference."

A huge group of employees, including Obadiah Stane, had gathered outside the main office tower at the campus headquarters of Stark Industries. They burst into applause as Tony's limo pulled up.

Pepper looked at her boss, worried, and helped him get out of the car.

Stane stepped forward and embraced Tony in a bear hug.

"Welcome home, boss," he said. Then, more quietly, so only Tony and Pepper could hear, he added, "I thought we were meeting at the hospital.

There are a lot of reporters here, waiting for you. What's going on?"

"You'll see," Tony said.

Tony leaned on Stane's shoulder, and the two of them walked into the building's main entrance. Pepper followed. Reporters packed the lobby from wall to wall.

Pepper didn't notice the man in the dark, tailored suit until he walked up behind her. He was tall, around forty, with a stern face and impeccably groomed hair.

"You'll have to take a seat, sir," Pepper said distractedly.

"I'm not a reporter," the man replied. "I'm Agent Phil Coulson, with the Strategic Homeland Intervention, Enforcement, and Logistics Division."

"That's a mouthful," Pepper said, her eyes not leaving Tony for a moment.

"I know," Coulson said, handing her his business card.

Pepper barely glanced at it. "Look, Mr. Coulson," she said, "we've already spoken with the D.O.D., the FBI, the CIA, the—"

"We're a separate division with a more . . . specific focus," Coulson said. "We need to debrief Tony about the circumstances of his escape."

"Well, that's great," Pepper said, cutting him off. "I'll let him know when he's got a free moment."

"We're here to help," Coulson insisted. "I assure you, Mr. Stark will want to talk to us."

"I'm sure he will," Pepper said. "Now, if you could just take your seat."

She walked away from the agent, moving through the crowd toward the podium. Tony looked shaky as he made his way to the microphones. Stane stayed by his side, ready to catch his boss if he staggered.

Tony stepped to the podium. For a moment, he looked like a deer frozen in headlights. But before Stane could step in, he composed himself and cleared his throat.

"I . . ." Tony began, "I can't do this any longer."

Silence. Finally, one of the reporters spoke up.

"You mean you're retiring?" he asked.

"No," Tony said. "I don't want to retire. I want to do something else."

Again, silence. "Something other than weapons?" the same reporter ventured.

Tony nodded. "Yes. That's right."

Stane gasped. The rest of the room buzzed. Reporters shouted questions over each other. Finally, one voice rose above the rest.

"The official report was sketchy, Mr. Stark," a reporter said. "What exactly happened to you over there?"

Tony looked thoughtful for a moment, and then

all his emotions seemed to overflow.

"What happened over there?" he repeated. "I had my eyes opened, that's what happened. I saw weapons with my name on them in the hands of insurgents. I thought we were doing good here. I can't say that anymore."

Rhodey sidled up to Pepper. "Weren't we taking him to the hospital?" he asked. She shrugged.

"What do you intend to do about it, Mr. Stark?" the second reporter asked.

"The system is broken," Tony said. "There's no accountability. As of this second, we are freezing sale of all Stark weaponry worldwide."

Obadiah Stane's jaw dropped, and the lobby erupted into chaos. Stane moved to cut Tony off.

"We've lost our way," Tony continued. "I need to reevaluate things. And my heart is telling me that I have more to offer the planet than blowing things up."

Tony put his arm around the flustered-looking Stane. "In the coming months," Tony said, "Mr. Stane and I will set a new course for Stark Industries. 'Tomorrow Today' has always been our slogan. It's time we try to live up to it."

Reporters shouted questions as Tony stepped back and Stane took the podium.

"Okay," Stane said. "What we should take away from this is that Tony's back, he's healthier than ever, and as soon as he heals up and takes some time off, we're going to have a little internal discussion and get back to you. Thank you for coming by."

Tony stepped off the stage, beaming. Pepper had never seen him so enthusiastic. He quickly worked his way through the crowd to where she and Rhodey were standing.

"Do you mean that?" Pepper asked. "Or is this some clever stock maneuver?"

"Wait and see," Tony replied. He headed out the side door and into the company's sprawling campus.

Stane found him near the ARK Reactor building.

"That went well," Stane said sarcastically.

"Did I just paint a target on my back?" Tony asked.

"Your back?" Stane replied. "What about *my* back? How much do you think our stock is going to drop tomorrow?"

Tony thought a moment. "Forty points."

"Minimum," Stane said, concerned. "Tony, we are a *weapons* manufacturer."

"I don't want war to be our only legacy," Tony said.

Stane frowned at him. "What we do here keeps the world from falling into chaos."

"Well, judging from what I've seen," Tony said,

"we're not doing a very good job. There are other things we can do."

"Like what?" Stane asked. "You want us to make baby bottles?"

"We could reopen development of Repulsor Technology," Tony mused.

"The ARK Reactor was a publicity stunt," Stane said. "We built it to shut up the hippies."

"It works," Tony observed.

"Yeah, as a science project," Stane replied. "It was never cost-effective. We knew that before we built it. Repulsor Technology is a dead end. Right?"

"Maybe," Tony replied.

Stane looked at him anxiously. "There haven't been any breakthroughs in thirty years. Right?"

Tony shook his head. "You're a lousy poker player, Obadiah. Who told you?"

"Come on," Stane said. "Let me see the thing."

"Was it Rhodey?" Tony asked.

"Just show it to me," Stane said.

Tony ripped open his shirt, revealing the glowing electronic unit in the middle of his chest.

"Well," Stane said, marveling, "everyone needs a hobby." He took a deep breath. "Listen, we're a team. There's nothing we can't do if we stick together. No more of this ready-*fire*-aim business. No more unplanned press conferences. Can you promise me that?"

"Maybe," Tony said.

Stane straightened up. "Let me handle this," he said. "I did it for your father; I'll do it for you, but, please, you just have to lay low for a while."

But "laying low" was never something Tony Stark was good at.

CHAPTER

The Stark Mansion came alive as Tony walked through the door. Jarvis, the house's computer system, turned on the lights, changed the color of the windows, switched the TV to Tony's favorite channel, and adjusted everything to Tony's preprogrammed preferences.

"Hello, Mr. Stark," said Jarvis's almost-human voice.

"Hello, Jarvis," Tony replied.

"What can I do for you, sir?"

"I need to build a better heart," Tony said.

"I'm not sure I follow, sir."

"Give me a scan and you'll see what I mean," Tony replied.

"Shall I prepare the scanner in the workshop, sir?" Jarvis asked.

"Please. I'll need a full analysis."

Less than twenty minutes later, Tony sat in the scanning booth in his lab. Laser beams and ultrasound imagers flashed over Tony's body, analyzing him from head to toe.

"Tell me your intentions for the RT device in your chest, sir," Jarvis said.

"It powers an electromagnet that keeps shrapnel from entering my heart," Tony replied. "Can you recommend any upgrades?"

"Why are you talking to me like a computer?" Jarvis asked, his electronic voice betraying not a hint of irony.

"Because you're acting like one," Tony replied.

"Shall I disable random pattern conversation?" Jarvis asked.

Tony sighed and buttoned his shirt. "No," he said. "It's okay. Despite the fact that you *are* a computer, you're the only one who understands me."

"I *don't* understand you, sir. But you did program me."

"Were you always this dry?" Tony asked. "I remember you having more personality than this."

"Should I activate sarcasm harmonics?"

"Fine. Could you please make your recommendations now?"

"It would thrill me to no end," Jarvis said.

A smile tugged at the corners of Tony's mouth. "Ah. That's more like it."

"Would you like them on-screen, or shall I talk for the next three-point-two hours?"

"On-screen would be great," Tony said.

A series of recommendations and schematics appeared on the lab's monitors. Tony studied them quickly, his keen mind taking in every detail.

"Great," he said. "Perfect. Just what I had in mind."

"Of course, sir," Jarvis said. "Shall I begin machining the parts?"

Tony loaded raw metal stock into the lab's Jarvis-controlled tools and began cutting the metal.

Half a world away, in the deserts of Afghanistan, a swarm of ragged men scoured the sand dunes, looking for items to scavenge.

"Over here! I found something!" one man called, pointing to a battered gauntlet protruding from the sand. He tugged the metal glove free and held it high, as though it were a trophy.

A corroded pickup truck bounced over the dunes toward the discovery. In the back of the truck stood a powerful man holding a mounted machine gun. A banner showing ten conjoined rings fluttered over the machine gunner's head.

The truck pulled up next to the discoverer and he threw the gauntlet into the back. He smiled up at the machine gunner's scarred and burned face, hoping for approval.

Raza, the scarred man, merely nodded.

"There's more here!" cried a man atop another dune.

"And here!" called another, farther on.

Raza picked up Iron Man's battered helmet from the truck bed and stared into the helmet's empty eye sockets. "Keep looking," he called to his men. "Bring me every piece of armor you find—no matter how small. I want all of it."

Pepper hung up on Agent Coulson for the third time—he was getting to be a real pest—and knocked on Tony's bedroom door. When no one answered, she poked her head inside. The bed was made but not slept in, though the TV was on. A finance advice show blared news about Stark Industries.

"I have one recommendation," the moderator was saying. "*Sell!* Abandon ship." Behind him, the day's newspaper headlines blazed across the screen—"Stark Raving Mad?" "Stark Lunacy," and other similar rants.

When Tony's voice came over the bedroom intercom, Pepper jumped. "Pepper, how big are your hands?" he asked.

Frowning, she hurried through the security doors and down to Tony's lab. When she arrived, she found the workshop dimly lit, dirty, and disorganized. Tony was sitting in a chair, shirtless, his chest plate glowing slightly.

Pepper steeled herself. Though she knew the device implanted in his chest had saved Tony's life, she still hadn't gotten used to it.

"I need you to help me," Tony said.

She stared at the glowing Repulsor-Tech device in his chest. "So that's the thing that's keeping you alive."

"That's the thing that *was* keeping me alive," he said. "It's now an antique. This is what *will* be keeping me alive for the foreseeable future." He held up a similar device that looked much more high-tech and powerful.

"Amazing," she said.

"I'm going to swap them out and switch all functions to the new unit," Tony said.

"Is it safe?" Pepper asked.

"Completely," he assured her. "First, I need you to reach in and—"

"Reach in to where?" she asked warily.

"The socket in my chest," Tony said. "Listen carefully, because we have to do this in a matter of minutes."

"Or else what?"

"I could go into cardiac arrest," Tony replied.

Pepper's stomach twisted into a knot. "I thought you said it was safe."

"I didn't want you to panic."

She felt the blood drain from her face.

"Stay with me," Tony said. "I'm going to lift off the old chest piece—"

"That won't kill you?"

"Not immediately. When I lift it off, I need you to reach into the socket. . . ." Tony kept talking, giving quick but complete directions so she could replace the unit.

Somehow, Pepper managed to get through the procedure without passing out. Afterward, she gazed at the old "heart" while one of the lab's robot arms finished installing the new unit.

"Can I wash my hands now?" she asked.

"Sure," he said, continuing to talk as she went to the sink. "The new unit is much more efficient. This shouldn't happen again."

"Good," she said, drying off, "because it's not in my job description."

"It is now," Tony replied.

She frowned at him and picked up the old unit. "What should I do with this?" she asked. The tiny power plant glowed slightly in her hand.

"That old thing?" Tony replied. "Throw it out."

Pepper frowned. "You made it out of spare

parts in a dungeon. It saved your life. Doesn't it at least have some nostalgic value?"

"Pepper," Tony said, "I have been called many things, but nostalgic is not one of them." The robot finished the installation of the new unit; the center of Tony's chest glowed brightly.

"There," Tony said. "Good as new. Thank you."

"You're welcome," Pepper said, feeling greatly relieved. "Can I ask you a favor? If you need some-one to do something like this again," she said, "get someone else."

"I don't have anyone else," Tony replied.

He looked into her eyes and, for a moment, she felt something for him she'd never felt before. She turned away. "Will that be all, Mr. Stark?"

"That will be all, Ms. Potts."

CHAPTER

10

Sketches and designs lay scattered across the worktable in Tony's lab as he tinkered with his newest invention—a pair of shining metal boots.

"Still having trouble walking, sir?" Jarvis asked.

"These aren't for walking," Tony replied.

He finished the adjustments, put the boots down, and marked a circle on the lab floor with electrical tape.

"Why are you marking up the floor?" the computerized butler asked.

"It's a test circle," Tony replied. "It'll help me gauge the experiment's success."

"I'll inform the cleaning staff," Jarvis said.

Tony put on the boots and stepped to the center of the circle. He draped a bandolier-like control device around his shoulders and hooked it all into his chest unit.

"Ready to record the big moment, Jarvis?" he asked, gripping the bandolier's joystick controls.

"All sensors ready, sir."

"We'll start off easy," Tony said. "Ten percent power." He pressed the activators on the joysticks.

Instantly, the boot jets fired and he shot toward the ceiling. He wrestled with the controls, flipped sideways, barely avoided the ceiling, and careened around the workshop before finally crashing into a pile of cardboard boxes in the corner.

As Tony lay upside down amid mounds of plastic packing material, Jarvis said, "That flight yielded excellent data, sir."

"Great," Tony replied.

Days later, Pepper came into the workshop as Tony fiddled with a pair of metal gauntlets. He put the gloves on, pointed them across the lab, and activated the Repulsor-Technology pads in the palms.

A blast of light issued forth from his hands. It hit a toolbox fifteen feet away, knocking it over and scattering the wrenches inside across the floor.

Pepper frowned. "I thought you were done inventing weapons," she said.

"It's not a weapon," Tony replied. "It's a flight stabilizer."

"Well, watch where you're pointing your flight stabilizer, would you?"

He gave a sheepish grin.

"Obadiah's upstairs," she said. "Should I tell him, you're in?"

"I'll be right up," Tony replied.

As she left, she placed a small box on the edge of his worktable. Intrigued, Tony took off the gauntlets and ripped the package open.

Inside was his old chest device, encased in Lucite. The reactor glowed faintly inside the clear plastic. Tony knew it would continue to glow for years. The casing had an inscription: PROOF THAT TONY STARK HAS A HEART. Tony chuckled and headed upstairs.

He reached the living room just as Obadiah Stane set a pizza down on the coffee table. Stane flashed the billionaire a concerned smile.

"Tony," Stane said, "how's it going?"

Tony paced the room, barely looking at the pizza. "This is big, Obadiah," he said. "The *big* idea. What I'm working on can pull the company in a whole new direction."

"That's great," Stane replied. "Get me the designs as soon as you can. We've got a hungry production line that can knock out a prototype in days."

Tony took a deep breath and looked at Obadiah.

"You know, I had a moment there where I was . . . worried," Tony said. "But now I know that I made the best decision. I feel like I'm doing something right . . . finally." He put his hand on Stane's shoulder. "Thank you for supporting all this."

Stane nodded, appearing genuinely touched. He took a deep breath, too.

"Listen," he said. "I have something to talk to you about. I really wish you'd attended the last board meeting like I asked you to."

"I know," Tony replied. "I'm sorry. What did I miss?"

"The board's filed an injunction against you."

Tony's jaw dropped. "What?"

"Tony, they claim you're unfit to run the company; they want to lock you out."

Tony began pacing again. "How can they do that? It's my name on the building—my ideas that run the company!"

"Well, they're going to try," Stane said. "We'll fight them, of course."

"With the amount of stock we own, I thought we controlled the company," Tony said.

Stane shook his head. "Somehow, they pulled enough votes together. The world doesn't share your vision, Tony. The more people have got to lose, the more frightened they are of new ideas."

Stane offered some pizza to Tony, but Tony declined.

"Now listen," Stane said, "I don't want you to get all tied in knots. You know how many times I protected your father from corporate wolves?"

Tony nodded, but he still felt worried.

"Get back to your lab and work some magic," Stane advised. "You let me handle the board."

"All right."

Stane stood. "Oh, and Tony. . . ?"

"Yes?"

"Please, no more unscheduled press conferences."

Tony nodded grimly and went back to the lab.

It took him a few more days to hook the boot units, the control bandolier, and the new gauntlets together. Once he'd done it, though, he couldn't resist trying out the setup.

"Shall I alert the rescue squad?" Jarvis asked as Tony fastened the last of the connections.

Tony flexed his arms. The tubing connecting the pieces felt stiff—but it was only a prototype, after all.

"No," Tony said. "I can handle this." He activated the boot jets and manipulated the controls.

Slowly, he rose off the floor and hovered in the air. The Repulsor stabilizers in the gloves kicked in, steadying his flight. He moved up in the air, holding his arms out like a tightrope walker.

After gaining his balance, he floated slowly around the room, dodging expensive pieces of electronic equipment and avoiding the cars, workbench, and other obstacles.

He nearly bumped his head on the ceiling twice and came perilously close to the roof of his Porsche, but he didn't hit anything. His papers and a few light objects scattered out of his way as he flew, repelled by the Repulsor forces powering the boots and the gauntlets.

"See?" he said. "Nothing to it."

He cut the propulsion, landed softly near his workbench, and grinned at one of Jarvis's sensors.

"All right," Tony said. "Now the real work begins."

Half a world away, Raza stared at the gray suit of armor being assembled on the lab table in his new hideout.

"Amazing," he muttered. Amazing that something like this could nearly destroy his whole operation.

It would be difficult to complete the reassembly without either Yinsen or Stark to guide his workers, but Raza knew the job would eventually get done.

And then he, Raza, would own a weapon that would be the envy of even the largest corporations and governments.

The warlord smiled and, for once, he did not mind the stiffness of his scarred face.

CHAPTER

11

Tony's metal boots clanked across the workshop floor. The armor felt heavy, so he made an adjustment to the servo-motors that powered it. His Repulsor-Technology heart glowed more brightly within his chest plate, and the suit moved more easily.

He flexed his arms and the suit flexed with him. The ailerons, air brakes, and other flying controls popped out on command, just as they were supposed to. The new armor covering him from head to toe felt good.

"Standby for calibration," he told Jarvis.

"Of course, sir," the computerized butler replied.

Tony fired up the boots and the gauntlet Repulsors. He rose into the air, hovered, and began to fly around the workshop. Then, suddenly, he lost his balance and plunged toward the floor.

He landed on his sports car, crushing the roof flat. The car's alarm system screamed in protest. Tony blasted the alarm with the Repulsor mounted in his palm. The alarm unit shook to pieces and went silent.

"A not entirely unsuccessful test," Jarvis observed.

Tony picked himself up, brushing stray bits of the automobile off his armor. "We should take this outside," he said.

"I must strongly caution against that," Jarvis warned. "There are terabytes of calculations still needed before the armor is fully operational and under control."

Behind his metal helmet, Tony smiled. "We'll do those calculations in flight."

"Sir," Jarvis said, "the suit has not even passed a basic wind-tunnel test."

"That's why you'll be making the flight with me," Tony replied.

He pressed a button on a lab console and downloaded Jarvis's program into the suit's computer system. The armor's heads-up display flashed to life.

Tony opened the workshop's garage doors and slowly hovered out the door and along the workshop driveway.

Jarvis's voice echoed in his helmet. "I suggest you allow me to employ Directive Four," the butler said.

Tony frowned, not remembering which directive that was. "Never interrupt me while I'm with a beautiful woman?" he guessed.

"That's Directive Six," Jarvis replied. "Directive Four is to use any and all means to protect your life, should you be incapable of doing so."

"Whatever," Tony replied. He kicked up the power and blasted into the night sky.

Iron Man weaved and wobbled through the air, trying to keep the horizon steady. He tried poses he'd seen in various movies, books, and comics about flying superheroes, but each one seemed more unstable than the previous one.

Then he had an idea. *You're jet powered,* he told himself. *Think like a jet.*

He thrust his chest out, held his chin up, kept his knees and feet together, and flung his arms out to the side—like a delta-winged fighter aircraft.

To his delight, the pose worked, and he zoomed through the air like a human missile. He pulled a few exhilarating banked turns, and then followed the ribbon of the Pacific Coast Highway south to Santa Monica. Onlookers gaped in awe as Iron Man buzzed the giant Ferris wheel on the pier.

Tony smiled and arced upward in a power

climb. The clouds streaked past like misty dreams. Soon he emerged into a perfect, starry night.

He was so high up now that the world seemed a tiny, distant place. Ice crystals formed on the inside of his helmet.

"Power: fifteen percent," Jarvis warned. "Recommend you descend and recharge, sir."

Caught up in the moment, Tony didn't listen. Instead, he zoomed ever higher, chasing the stars.

"Mr. Stark," Jarvis said, "please acknowledge."

The moon beckoned before him, huge and impossibly bright. Tony never remembered seeing anything more beautiful in his life.

"Power at five percent," Jarvis warned. "Threshold breached—"

Suddenly, the heads-up display inside Tony's helmet went dark. One remaining warning light flashed: SYSTEM SHUTDOWN.

Iron Man's thrusters sputtered and died. The suit felt heavy and awkward. Tony glanced at his chest plate; it wasn't glowing.

The weight of the armor overcame his momentum and he plummeted, pinwheeling toward the earth.

"Uh, Jarvis?" Tony called. "Jarvis!"

The earth zoomed up toward him.

"Status!" Tony called to the silent computer system. "Status! Reboot!"

Tony Stark,
billionaire and inventor.

When Stark is captured by insurgents, he must invent a way to escape.

A new hero takes shape. Stark welds an iron suit together.

Iron Man is born.

Remnants of the first suit fall into the wrong hands.

The insurgents try to piece together the puzzle.

Back home, Stark catches up with his assistant, Pepper Potts.

Locked away in his workshop, Stark builds a new suit of Iron Man armor.

Lieutenant Colonel Rhodes worries about his best friend's new obsession.

Pepper Potts is also worried for Stark's safety.

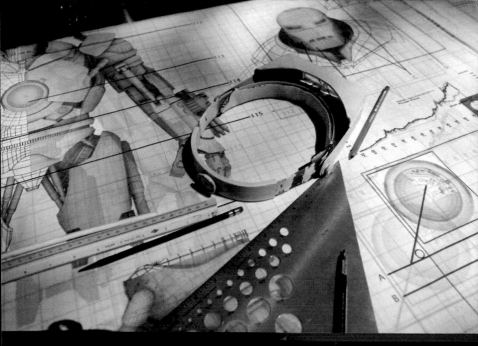

The drawings of the Iron Man suit are stolen
and used to build a bigger weapon . . .

. . . Iron Monger.

Iron Man is
ready for battle.

Will Iron Man save the day?

He plummeted through the clouds. The coast-line appeared below, the lights of the city blazed into view, and the snaking curve of the highway revealed itself.

Why hadn't he listened to Jarvis?

Something popped near his ear and, suddenly, the heads-up display flickered back to life. Power surged through the suit's servo-motors and cir-cuits. Tony fought to bring the armor back under control.

"Temporary power restored," Jarvis said calmly. "Descend immediately."

Tony righted himself and flew back toward the mansion. He aimed for the driveway, struggling to maintain stability.

"Shall I take over the final descent?" Jarvis asked.

"No," Tony said proudly. "I've got it. I—"

An accidental shift of his weight sent him crashing through the roof of the mansion.

Shattered beams and plaster rained around him as he broke through the ceiling of his garage and landed on top of another sports car.

The impact shook his entire body and set off every car alarm in the garage. Annoyed, Tony scrambled to his feet and pulled off his helmet.

"Shall I alert the body shop, sir?" Jarvis asked.

"No," Tony replied. "Just switch the alarms off

and let security know we've had a little . . . set-back."

"Very good, sir," Jarvis said.

"Perfect," Tony replied. "Now let's do some upgrades."

He clambered out of the armor and hung it on the work rack nearby, then began typing design notes into his computer. Graphics and data scrolled down the lab's many monitors.

"That venture was quite dangerous," Jarvis noted as Tony continued to work. "Might I remind you, if the suit loses power, so does your heart."

"And the armor doesn't have a seat belt, either," Tony replied. "A few issues: main transducer felt sluggish at plus forty altitude. Same goes for hull pressurization. I think the icing might have been a factor."

"This design isn't rated for high altitude," Jarvis observed. "You're expending eight percent power just heating and pressurizing."

"Reconfigure the suit using the gold-titanium alloy from the Seraphim Tactical Satellite. It should ensure fuselage integrity to fifty thousand feet while still maintaining power-to-weight ratio."

"Shall I simulate a new hull utilizing the pro-posed specifications on screen?" Jarvis asked.

"Wow me."

On-screen, the sleek form of the Mark II armor

transformed into an even sleeker, golden Mark III prototype.

Tony regarded it and rubbed his chin. "A bit . . . *ostentatious,* isn't it?" He glanced over at his collection of cars and motorcycles, seeking inspiration in their paint jobs.

"Add a little red, would you?" he said, pointing to the screen. "Here, here, and here." The computer graphics prototype changed color appropriately.

Just then, Tony noticed the image on the television, which had been playing silently in the background. He turned up the volume.

A local reporter stood outside a grand entertainment hall where a huge crowd was gathering. "Tonight's red-hot red carpet is here at the Concert Hall, where Tony Stark's annual benefit for the Firefighter Family Fund has become the go-to charity gala on L.A.'s high-society calendar."

Tony noticed a flashing reminder from Pepper about the event on his computer screen, and slapped his head. Nearby, the lab's automated tooling and manufacturing machines sprang to life.

"But this great cause is only part of the story," the reporter continued. "The man whose name graces the gold-lettered invitations to the event hasn't been seen in public since his highly controversial press conference, and rumors about him abound. Some say Stark is suffering from post-traumatic stress disorder and hasn't left his bed in weeks."

Tony scoffed and returned his attention to the design screen. The red-and-gold Iron Man Mark III uniform looked good—very good.

"The work could take until morning to complete, sir," Jarvis noted.

"Good," Tony said. "I should come up for air anyway. Pick me out an undamaged car, would you? I need to change before I go to that benefit."

CHAPTER

The crowd outside the concert hall filled the entire avenue and overflowed into the surrounding streets. The concertgoers were a mix of celebrities, generals, business tycoons, and movie stars.

Flashbulbs lit the scene as Tony pulled his sports car up to the curb. He got out, waved to the crowd, and handed his keys to the waiting valet.

The crowd roared as Tony stepped onto the red carpet and, for just a moment, the former prisoner-of-war felt completely out of place. Not so long ago, these had been *his* people, but now they were just a sea of faces.

Just then, Obadiah Stane appeared at his elbow. "Excuse us a moment, would you?" Stane said, steering Tony away from the crowd.

"Hi, Obadiah," Tony said. "What's the big rush?"

"What are you doing here?" Stane asked, looking nervous. "I thought you were going to lay low."

Tony shrugged. "It's time to start showing my face again."

"Let's just take it slow, okay?" Stane said. "I've got the board right where we want them." He nodded toward a group of Stark Industries executives milling around with the red carpet crowd.

"Great," Tony replied, giving the board members a curt wave. "Look, I'll see you inside." He headed for the theater doors, anxious not to get caught up in company business.

The interior of the venue was almost as crowded as outside. Music filled the concert hall as happy couples whirled around the dance floor. Tony spotted Pepper coming down the stairs. She looked stunning in a classic evening gown.

Tony made a beeline for her. She looked surprised and pleased to see him.

"Ms. Potts," Tony said, "can I have five minutes? You look . . . like you should *always* wear that dress."

"Thanks," she said. "It was a birthday present—from you."

"I have great taste," Tony said. "Care to dance?" He took her hand and whisked her onto the dance floor. She looked away from him bashfully.

"I'm sorry," Tony said. "Am I making you uncomfortable?"

"No," she replied, her face slightly flushed. "I always wear a chiffon dress, forget to put on deodorant, and dance with my boss in front of everyone I've ever worked with."

"Would it help if I fired you?" Tony asked.

She grinned. "You wouldn't last a week without me."

"I might," Tony said.

"What's your Social Security number?" she asked.

"Uh . . . ," Tony began.

She whispered it into his ear.

Tony chuckled. "I guess I wouldn't make it on my own after all."

They danced together long enough that Tony lost track of time. Finally, they retired to the veranda outside to catch their breaths. Pepper looked beautiful in the starlight.

They stood silently for a moment. "Can I get you something to drink?" Tony finally asked.

"Yes, please," she said.

Tony went and picked up a pair of drinks from the buffet table. Before he could return to Pepper, though, reporter Christine Everhart strode up to him. She had a file folder under her arm.

"Mr. Stark," she said, shoving a microphone into his face, "I was hoping I could get a reaction from you on your company's involvement in this latest atrocity," she said.

"Hey, I didn't set up this event," Tony explained, loosening his collar. "They just put my name on the invitation to draw more people."

She opened the file folder and thrust it toward him. Inside, there were pictures of Ten Rings separatists clutching Stark machine guns, rocket-propelled grenade launchers, and other weapons. Behind them, a village burned.

Tony looked at the photos, and his blood ran cold. "When were these taken?" he asked.

"Yesterday," she replied. "Good public relations move. You tell the world you're a changed man, but continue doing business as usual."

"I didn't approve this shipment," Tony said. He felt as though the world was crumbling around him.

"Well, your company did," Christine replied.

Tony took her by the hand. "Come with me," he said. Together, the two of them strode out of the building to where the huge mass of reporters stood, waiting to take pictures of celebrities leaving the event.

Outpacing Ms. Everhart, Tony found the biggest mass of cameras and microphones and stopped in front of them. "I made some promises I'm not going to be able to keep," he began. "I suggest you pull all your money out of Stark Industries immediately, and—"

Instantly, Obadiah Stane dashed up next to him. He grabbed Tony's elbow and hustled him away from the reporters.

"Is this some kind of nervous tic for you?" Stane hissed when they made their way to the back of the building. "Whenever you have a twinge of conscience, you hold a press conference? Those people are going to put a negative spin on everything you say!"

Tony stopped dead in his tracks. "Wait a minute," he said. "I need to ask you something. I'm dead serious about this. Am I losing my mind, or is Pepper really cute? I've been out of the game for a while, so I'm not sure."

Stane shook his head and stared at Tony in disbelief. "How can you talk about women after doing what you just did?" Stane asked. "Maybe you *are* out of your mind. You're messing with the 'guys in the rooms.' We're talking about billion-dollar interests, the world order, and—"

"I'm not worried about that right now," Tony said.

"You *should be* worried," Stane shot back. "You'll disappear. Even with all your money, it could happen. I can't protect you against people that powerful. Don't be so naive."

"Naive?" Tony said. "When I was growing up, they told me there were lines I couldn't cross because that's how we did business. But in the meantime, Stark Industries is double-dealing under the table. Our company doesn't deserve to represent the United States."

"Tony," Stane said, "you're acting like a child."

Tony gazed into Stane's eyes and saw fear. "You don't believe I can turn this company around," Tony said. "You think we'll go broke unless we sell weapons."

"Tony, you've got about as much control over our business as a child riding in the backseat of your father's car holding a red plastic steering wheel in your hand."

"Maybe I'll just get out of the car," Tony replied.

"You're not even allowed *in* the car," Stane said. He took a deep breath. "I'm the one who's filing the injunction against you."

Tony couldn't believe it. Stane turned and walked away, but Tony caught up to him.

He grabbed Stane by the jacket and spun him around. "Why?" Tony asked angrily.

"It's the only way I could protect you," Stane

replied. As he said it, two large bodyguards stepped between him and Tony. With a final shake of his head, Stane left the party and climbed into his waiting limousine.

CHAPTER

13

Tony sat hunched over his workbench, wearing a prototype of the Mark III Iron Man gauntlet. On the wall beside him, a large flat-screen TV monitor blared with the latest news.

The TV showed long lines of refugees streaming out of the ruins of Gulmira as triumphant Ten Rings separatists ran rampant through Gulmira City. It seemed that Raza's rebel group was spreading beyond Afghanistan.

Tony aimed the gauntlet at a hanging light fixture twenty feet away and activated the Repulsor unit. The lights sparked and fizzled and fell from the ceiling.

The scene on the TV switched, now showing half-starved refugees gathered in makeshift camps and caves in the Gulmira hills. In the midst of the crowd, a starving child wept.

Tony adjusted the gauntlet, raising the power level. He pointed it toward a window on the far side of the lab and fired. The blast shattered the glass and knocked a nearby picture off the wall.

"With no international political will or pressure," the TV reporter concluded, "there is little hope for these newly displaced refugees— refugees who can only wonder one thing: Is the world watching?"

Tony made a final adjustment to the gauntlet and blasted the TV to smithereens. As silence descended over the lab, he nodded in satisfaction.

Pepper appeared at the doorway. She looked over the destruction and shook her head. "Are you going to tell me what's going on?" she asked.

"Get my house in Dubai ready," Tony replied. "I want to throw a party."

Pepper spoke through gritted teeth. "Yes, Mr. Stark."

Tony's villa in Dubai wasn't nearly as opulent as his Pacific Coast mansion, but it was still enough to make a millionaire green with envy. A long line of expensive cars pulled up in the driveway, dropping off expensively clothed passengers. Multicolored, pulsating light flooded out of the house, and throbbing music filled the hot night air.

Tony wove through the glittering guests, slapping shoulders, shaking hands, and making small talk. By the time he bumped into Pepper, he had a beautiful woman on each arm.

"Well," she said frostily, "you seem back in old form."

"Life of the party," he said. "Isn't that what everyone wanted?" He smiled at her, but she didn't smile back. The two girls that were with him giggled. "Cue the fireworks in five, would you, Pepper?" he said.

"Sure," she hissed. "Don't hurt yourself."

Tony nodded at her and walked away. It took him a few minutes to ditch the girls, and a few more to suit up in his new armor.

"Time for a test flight," he mused as the show began outside.

Using the fireworks as cover, he streaked into the night sky. A backward glance as he left revealed Pepper standing, alone, near the property's beach. She looked sad.

For a moment, Tony felt guilty for leaving her behind to tend to his guests. Then he set his onboard navigation system for Gulmira.

Fire lit up Gulmira City as he arrived. Gunshots and explosions filled the darkness. Black-clad Ten Rings rebels patrolled among the hovels and refugee tents on the outskirts of the city.

A boy not more than twelve years old darted through an alleyway, clutching a puppy in his arms. He didn't see the four separatists in the square until he almost ran into them. The men shouted and raised their weapons; the boy cowered, knowing he was doomed.

Iron Man dropped out of the night sky, landing between the rebels and their intended victim. Tony slammed his fist into the ground and the armor intensified the power of his punch a thousandfold.

The street shattered, hurling the enemy soldiers into the air.

Iron Man scooped the child into his arms and flew the boy and puppy to safety. By the time Tony returned, an enemy jeep, flying the Ten Rings flag, had arrived in the square.

"Raza's men!" Tony said to himself.

They fired at him as he landed in the square. The bullets bounced off Iron Man's improved armor without even making a dent. Tony powered up the Repulsor units in his gloves. He fired, knocking out a dozen men and overturning their jeep with the first burst.

The rest charged, coming at him from both front and rear. Tony swung his fist and sent the four in front sprawling.

One soldier grabbed him from behind. Iron Man reached back and lifted the man into the air with one hand. As the soldier screamed for mercy, Tony hurled him into three more of his comrades, bowling them over like tenpins.

Inside his helmet, Tony Stark smiled.

Then, without warning, something struck him hard in the back. The crack of a sniper rifle echoed across the square. Tony swept the area with his infrared sensors and spotted the sniper's heat signature on a nearby rooftop.

Iron Man whirled and fired his Repulsors at the sniper, but the blast had no effect. A message flashed on Tony's heads-up display: OUT OF RANGE.

Another shot hit Iron Man's shoulder. The armor didn't dent, but the impact rocked Tony again. He stumbled back against the overturned jeep. The tire pressing into his back gave him an idea.

Iron Man ripped the wheel off the vehicle and spun in a circle, holding the tire like a discus. His heads-up display calculated angles and trajectories.

At just the right moment, he let go of the tire. It soared through the air in a graceful arc and knocked the sniper out cold.

But before Iron Man could enjoy the victory, a tank shell shattered the building next to him. Tony staggered as tons of bricks and mortar rained down on his armor. The refugees, who had crept out of hiding to watch Iron Man, scurried back to safety.

Then the tank itself rumbled into view, knocking down makeshift hovels as it came. It trained its turret cannon toward Iron Man as he rose to his feet.

Tony studied the tank's schematic on his heads-up display. The tank was Stark designed, and his computer files showed him everything about it, including its weaknesses.

The tank fired again, but Iron Man was already moving. A mini-missile launcher popped open on Tony's left gauntlet.

Iron Man fired the missile into the tank, hitting it between the body and turret. The tank's systems overloaded and, moments later, its passengers jumped to safety as the tank exploded.

Tony's heads-up display showed someone coming up behind him. He whirled, Repulsors ready to blast the enemy into next week.

But it was only a child—the same boy Tony had rescued earlier. In his outstretched hand, the boy held an apple.

Iron Man mussed the boy's hair affectionately and then took to the sky once more. He looked around and saw no more rebels prowling the streets. The refugees below cheered. Heaving a sigh of relief, Tony said, "Jarvis, plot a course for home."

• • •

"So, who's behind the robotic whatzit causing this ruckus in Gulmira?" Major Allen asked Lieutenant Colonel Rhodes.

"I don't think it's Russian," Rhodey replied. "Or Chinese."

Major Allen frowned. "Then where did it come from?"

Rhodey thought a moment and then said, "Let me make a call." He picked up a phone and punched in Tony Stark's private number. A moment later, Tony's voice came over the earpiece.

"Yeah?"

Rhodey could barely hear him; it was a terrible connection. "Tony, it's Rhodey. What's that noise?"

"I'm in the convertible," Tony replied. "Look, this isn't the best time—"

"I need a quick ID," Rhodey said, studying the ongoing satellite pictures. "What do you know about unmanned combat robotics with air-to-ground capabilities?"

"I've never heard of anything like that," Tony said.

Rhodey covered the phone's receiver as the control officer said, "The unmanned arial vehicle has entered the no-fly zone."

"Why do you ask?" Tony continued, oblivious to the announcement.

"Because I think I'm staring at one right now," Rhodey said, "and it's about to get blown to kingdom come."

An alarm blared in the control room, announcing that the Unmanned Arial Vehicle, called a UAV, was violating the patrolled airspace.

"Rhodes!" Allen barked. "You got something for me?"

Rhodes looked from the major to the phone, caught between conversations.

"Uh . . . kingdom come?" Tony asked.

"Scramble those F-22s," Major Allen ordered. "The jets will deal with that thing, whatever it is."

Tony looked up as two U.S. Air Force F-22 Raptors streaked out of the sky toward him.

"This is my exit," he said, lying to Rhodey. "I gotta go." He switched off the phone link inside his helmet.

The jets screamed ahead, gaining on him. Tony turned on the armor's turbo booster and shot forward. He pulled into a tight bank, but the planes remained on his tail.

Beads of sweat rolled down Tony's back. Every time he turned, the planes turned with him. His heads-up display showed their weapons systems trying to lock on. He knew it wouldn't be long before they had him in their sights.

But would they fire? He was on their side, after all.

Of course, they didn't know that.

"Pursuing aircraft have locked on," Jarvis announced calmly.

Tony glanced back over his shoulder as the lead jet fired a missile at him.

14

The missile streaked straight toward Iron Man. In his revamped armor, Tony was as fast as the jets—but the sidewinder missile was faster still.

Tony concentrated, sending every iota of power he could into the suit's thrusters but, each moment, his heads-up-display showed the missile gaining on him.

Jarvis's voice remained calm. "Incoming sidewinder in five . . . four . . . three . . . two . . ."

Tony activated the suit's counter measures. Instantly a hatch popped open, and big, confettilike flakes of metal burst into the air.

The sidewinder hit the chaff and exploded. The fireball from the explosion surrounded Iron Man, but Tony didn't even feel it through the armor.

Unfortunately, the F-22 jets hadn't given up yet.

Iron Man dived toward the ground, rolled to his left, banked right. The Raptors followed close behind.

Tony flew as fast as he could, trying to keep the jets from locking on again. He banked into a hard turn. The g-force meter inside his helmet went from green to yellow to red. The world around him blurred, and Tony nearly blacked out.

"Sir," Jarvis said, "may I remind you that the suit can handle these maneuvers, but *you* cannot."

The F-22s sprayed machine-gun fire into Iron Man's path.

White-hot tracer rounds streaked past Tony, exploding and ricocheting off his armor. For the first time, the new suit buckled and tore.

Tony grimaced and said, "Jarvis—air brakes!"

Instantly, all of the suit's drag-inducing flaps opened, slowing Iron Man to a halt in seconds. Tony grunted as g-forces pressed him against the inside of the suit.

The jets shot past Iron Man, twin blurs of aviation gray. Tony breathed a sigh of relief. The Raptors would be miles away before they could turn back on him again.

"Jarvis," he said, "get Rhodey on the line."

The computerized butler put the call through.

"Tony?" Rhodey's voice said.

"Rhodey, I had Jarvis run a check," Tony replied. "I might have some info on that UAV. A piece of gear like that might exist. Might *definitely* exist."

Rhodey's voice came back hushed, as though he didn't want the people with him to overhear. "It wouldn't happen to be red and gold, would it?"

The jets turned and screamed back toward Tony.

"The color doesn't matter," Tony said. "What matters is that it would definitely be on *our* side."

Tony dived down low so the jets' radar would have trouble picking him out against the terrain on the ground.

"And what do you expect me to do?" Rhodey asked.

"Call off the dogs?" Tony asked hopefully.

"I think it's a little late for that," Rhodey replied.

"I was afraid you'd say that," Tony said. He switched off the phone. "Jarvis, I want to hear the communications channel for those jets."

"At once, sir."

As the jets screamed past overhead, Iron Man shot up from the ground and clamped onto the belly of the closest one. Unfortunately, it only took a moment for the Raptor's wingman to notice.

"Viper One, he's on your belly," the second jet's pilot called.

"What?" Viper One asked, seemingly unable to believe it.

"He's clinging to your belly! Shake him off!"

The F-22 Raptor immediately began a series of swoops, dives, and turns. Even with his armor-enhanced fingers, Tony barely hung on. The maneuvers shook him inside the suit like nails inside a tin can.

"Headquarters," Viper Two said, "that is definitely *not* a UAV."

A voice Tony recognized as Major Allen came over the speaker. "What is it, then?" Allen asked.

"I think it's a . . . it's a man, sir."

"Viper Two," Viper One said, "it's still there. Roll! Roll!"

Tony clung tight as the airplane began a series of dizzying rolls, twists, and spins—up, down, sideways, and back again. Inside his armor, Tony began to feel queasy.

"Sir," Jarvis's calm voice said, "in two minutes we won't have sufficient power to return home."

Iron Man lost his grip and tumbled through the air. He smashed into Viper Two's tail fin, ripping it off. The jet careened toward the ground.

"I'm hit!" Viper Two cried. He pushed the eject button and the canopy of his aircraft flew off. The rocket-powered cockpit chair zoomed clear of the crippled aircraft, but the chair's parachute failed to open.

"Viper One," Major Allen called, "do you see a chute?"

"Negative!" Viper One replied. "No chute! No chute!"

Iron Man streaked forward, angling for the falling pilot.

"Power *critical*," Jarvis intoned. "Set course for home immediately."

"The UAV is going after him!" Viper One cried. "It's attacking!"

The heads-up display gave Tony the information he needed. He rocketed toward the falling pilot. At the last instant, Iron Man's metal fingers found the jammed chute mechanism and ripped it open.

The pilot's chute deployed with a loud whooshing sound. The parachute caught the air and jerked the pilot upward, away from Iron Man. The chute billowed out, gliding the pilot safely toward earth.

Beneath his helmet, Tony grinned.

"Good chute! Good chute!" Viper One called. "You're not going to believe this, but that UAV just saved his life!"

Iron Man fired his thrusters, banking sharply, and barely avoided slamming into the ground. Viper One executed a barrel roll and came up right on his tail.

"Viper One," Major Allen called, "reengage."

"Wait!" Rhodey's voice blurted over the open channel.

"Take the target out!" Allen ordered.

Nearly every system in Tony's armor was flashing CRITICAL. He didn't have the power for any more fancy maneuvers; he barely had the power to make it back home.

"Major," Rhodey said, "call off that Raptor. You don't know what you're shooting at."

"We'll find out when we recover the pieces," Major Allen replied.

"Jet's targeting system has locked on, sir," Jarvis warned.

"Headquarters," Viper One called, "you want me to engage the UAV?"

"Copy that," Major Allen said. "That thing just took out an F-22 inside a legal no-fly zone. Viper One, if you get a clean shot, you take it!"

"Roger," Viper One replied.

A missile dropped away from under the jet's wing and streaked toward Iron Man. Tony braced himself for the impact.

Rhodey's frantic voice cut in over the radio. "Negative!" he commanded. "Viper One, disengage!"

The next instant . . . WHOOM! The missile exploded.

15

Pepper sat on a small couch inside Tony's Dubai villa, her head propped in her hands. The guests had left long ago, but, strangely, she could find no sign of Tony. Hours ago, she had decided to wait up for his return. But she was dozing now, exhausted from the party.

A sudden whooshing sound startled her awake. The house shook, as though something very heavy had fallen over in the bedroom.

Pepper opened the door to the room. A figure sat in the bedroom's biggest chair. He was barely visible in a cloud of smoke.

It was Tony, wearing a suit of armor. The armor was scarred and pitted, as though it had been in a terrible battle. Tony held a battered metal helmet in his hands.

"They nearly got me," he gasped. "Please, Pepper, get me home."

A train of black SUVs wound through the desert toward Raza's hideout. The vehicles stopped near the warlord's tent, and private security guards stepped out. They took up defensive positions around the convoy.

Obadiah Stane stepped from his SUV as warlord Raza pulled back the tent flaps.

"Welcome," Raza said. Seeing Stane's gaze linger on his scarred face, he added, "Compliments of Tony Stark."

"If you'd killed him when you were supposed to," Stane said, "you'd still have a face."

Raza's smile turned into a savage grimace. "You paid us trinkets to kill a prince," the warlord said. "An insult, both to me and to the lord whose ring I wear." He held up his hand, showing the symbol of Ten Rings, interlocked, on the one ring he wore.

"I think it is best we don't get your master involved in this," Stane said. "I've come a long way to see this weapon. Show me."

Raza nodded. "Come. Leave your guards outside."

Stane entered the tent and stared. The weapon was gray, human-sized, and hanging from wires near the rear of the yurt. It resembled a high-tech suit of medieval armor. It was scarred and pitted, nearly destroyed before being pieced back together.

"Stark's escape bore unexpected fruit," Raza said.

Stane nodded slowly. "So *this* is how he did it."

"This is only a crude first effort," Raza said. "From what my men tell me of their recent battle, I believe Stark has perfected the design."

He handed Stane a set of grainy surveillance photos showing a man in red and gold armor wreaking havoc in Gulmira. Two of Raza's men brought in a battered laptop and reams of yellowed paper filled with drawings and schematics.

"What's this?" Stane asked.

"The inside of Tony Stark's mind," Raza replied. He shuffled the papers around until they fit together like a giant jigsaw puzzle. The puzzle revealed the form of Iron Man.

"These contain everything you will need to build this weapon," Raza said as Stane studied the plans. "Stark has made a masterpiece of death. A man with a dozen of these could rule from the Pacific to the Ukraine. You dream of Stark's throne, Mr. Stane. It seems we have a common enemy."

Stane ran his fingers over the armor, putting his hand through the hole in the chest plate.

"If we are back in business," Raza said, "I give you these designs as my gift. In turn, I hope you will repay me with the gift of iron soldiers."

Stane smiled and put his hands on Raza's shoulders.

"Take this gift as advance payment," Stane said.

For a moment, Raza looked puzzled. Then he collapsed to the ground, a victim of Stane's hidden sonic Taser. Stane removed the earplugs that had protected him from the device's effects.

"Technology has always been your Achilles' heel, Raza," Stane said. "Don't worry. The Taser's stunning effect will wear off in fifteen minutes. But by then, you'll have other problems."

He glanced at the ring on Raza's hand. "It'll be pretty hard for you to explain this to your master."

Stane turned and exited the tent. As expected, his men had easily rounded up Raza's troops. The warlord's men knelt, bound and gagged, near the SUVs.

"Crate up the armor and everything else in there," Stane told his lead guard. "We're taking it with us."

Pepper hung up on Agent Coulson again, as someone buzzed the doorbell of the Stark mansion in California. She checked the security monitor and saw Rhodey at the front door.

"Pepper, it's Rhodey."

She deactivated the computer-controlled lock and said, "Come in."

"How's Tony doing?" Rhodey asked.

She shook her head. "Not so good."

Rhodey glanced toward the still-unrepaired hole in the living room ceiling and looked even more concerned. "What is going on here?" he asked. "Let me in there, Pepper."

He moved toward the bedroom door, but she blocked his way. She glared at him, furious. "You want to see him?" she said. "Fine. See what you've done to him!"

She stepped back and Rhodey pushed through the door. His eyes went wide as he saw Tony, lying in bed, connected to a mass of wires and high-tech machines.

Rhodey sat down in an upholstered chair next to Tony. "Look at you," he muttered. "What were you thinking?"

Tony's eyes flickered open. "Weapons I built are being used to kill innocent people," he said. "I can't let that happen anymore."

"You can't go around and blow up stuff every time you see something you don't like on TV," Rhodey said.

"Yes I can," Tony replied.

"You got lucky," Rhodey said, concerned. "Next

time, they'll blow you to pieces."

A wry grin broke over Tony's bandaged face. "Maybe next time I won't play defense." His eyelids began to droop.

"You've put me in a tough spot here," Rhodey said. "What am I supposed to do?"

"That's up to you," Tony replied sleepily. "I've made my choice. I'm not going to sit on the sidelines anymore. I'm going to fight for what's right."

"Don't you get it?" Rhodey said angrily. "It's not up to *us* to decide!"

Tony closed his eyes. "That's where you're wrong."

In a subbasement of Stark Industries, Obadiah Stane spoke to a group of the company's best engineers. Before them sat Iron Man's old, gray armor, disassembled into its component pieces.

As the engineers worked to replicate the armor's parts, Stane walked among them, supervising.

"Give us full access to the Sampson Cluster development tools, and we'll have you a prototype in record time," the head engineer told him.

Stane nodded. "The Sampson's yours," he said. "We go twenty-four seven until the prototype is done."

"There's only one problem," the engineer noted.

"What's that?" asked Stane.

"There's no technology in the world that can power this thing."

"I told you," Stane said with exasperation, "miniaturize the ARK Reactor."

The engineer shook his head. "I'm sorry, Mr. Stane. I've tried. What you're asking for can't be done."

Stane glared at him. "Tony Stark was able to do it in a cave, with a box of scrap parts."

"Well," the engineer said, "I'm not Tony Stark."

"Keep working," Stane ordered. "We'll make it happen—somehow."

CHAPTER

16

Deeming himself sufficiently healed, Tony unplugged himself from life support and went down to his lab. Four hours later, he took a finger-sized gadget from his worktable and handed it to Pepper.

"This device will hack into the Stark Industries mainframe," he told her. "I need you to go there and retrieve all the shipping manifests."

"Absolutely not," Pepper replied. "You should be in bed, recuperating."

Tony shook his head. "They've been dealing weapons under the table, and I'm going to stop them."

"I'm not helping you if you're going to start this again," she said.

"There *is* nothing else," Tony said. "There's no

art opening, no benefit, no business decision to be made. There's the next mission and nothing else."

"I quit," Pepper said.

Tony arched an eyebrow at her. "Really? You stood by my side when all I did was reap the benefits of wholesale destruction, and now that I'm trying to right those wrongs and protect the people I put in harm's way, you're going to walk out on me?"

"You're going to kill yourself," she said. "I can't support that."

"Pepper, I know what I have to do. I don't know if I can, but I know in my heart that it's right. You do, too. And I can't do it without you."

Slowly, Pepper nodded.

Pepper hurried through the darkened halls of Stark Industries. She knew the corridors like the back of her hand. But sneaking around for Tony made her nervous.

Fortunately, she hadn't run into anyone on her way to Tony's office. She turned on his computer and plugged in the device he'd given her.

The gadget quickly began hacking into all the computers in the network. As it worked, she packed some of her personal things into a box. If she was going to be working at Tony's house for a while, she'd need her stuff.

The hacking device quickly located Obadiah Stane's machine and began downloading information from his hard drive. Pepper's eyes went wide as orders for Jericho missiles, shipping manifests, schematics, and blueprints flashed on the screen.

"What are you doing, Obadiah?" she asked quietly.

An icon for a video file appeared onscreen. She clicked it open and watched as the image sprang to life.

The picture showed Tony, very beaten up, tied to a chair in a cave. Thuggish-looking guards surrounded him. One of the guards spoke.

"Obadiah Stane, you have deceived us," the brutish man said. "The price to kill Tony Stark has just gone up."

Pepper's jaw dropped. Just then, the office door opened, and Stane walked in.

"What a nice surprise," he said, circling around the desk to greet her. As he did, she quickly switched the computer screen to a harmless search engine.

"How's Tony?" Stane asked.

"Honestly," she said, "I don't know. He's shut me out."

Stane nodded understandingly. "You and everyone else."

He picked up a picture of Tony's father from

the desk and shook his head.

"This . . . problem between you and Tony," Pepper said, "it's hurting him. You're the only real father Tony ever had. It would mean so much if you could just talk—"

"Tony's imploding," Stane said, putting the picture down. "It's unfortunate. You should consider whether you want to take that ride with him."

"Unfortunate?" Pepper asked.

"You know I love Tony," Stane said, "but this is business. We can't save him, but we can save his legacy." He had circled around to the front of the desk once more—out of view of the monitor and the device.

Pepper glanced down at the gadget. It read, 87% completed.

"It's tragic," Stane continued, "but Tony never really came home from Afghanistan, did he? This company has a bright future, Pepper. I'd like you to be part of it. Tony doesn't understand your value. He never did."

She surreptitiously checked the gadget and, finding the downloads complete, casually switched off the computer. "Are you offering me a job?" she asked.

"Think about it," he said, picking up the box she'd been packing. "Come on. I'll see you out."

She nodded and, as he turned away, she

snatched the hacking device from the computer. Just at that moment, Stane glanced back.

Pepper watched him nervously as they made their way to the building's main entrance. Had he seen? Did he know she was spying on him? Just when she thought he might accuse her, they ran into Agent Coulson at the security desk.

"Ms. Potts," Coulson said, "did you forget our appointment?"

"No," Pepper replied, latching onto his arm. "Of course not. I've been very much looking forward to it." She took her box of possessions from Stane. "Why don't we talk . . . somewhere else."

As she led Coulson out of the building, Stane hurried off in the opposite direction.

Tony Stark left his workshop and found Obadiah Stane in the Stark mansion living room, holding a pizza box. "Four cheese," Stane announced. I just had it flown in from Chicago." He set the pizza box down on the coffee table and handed Tony a letter.

"I'd like you to proofread something for me," Stane said.

"Would you like me to spell-check it, sir?" Jarvis offered.

"Can you turn him off?" Stane asked. "All the way off? I'd like to keep this private."

Tony took the letter and nodded. "Spin down,

Jarvis," he said, scanning the letter. What he read puzzled him. "Your resignation?" he asked.

"You were right," Stane replied. "It's not my company—not my name on the building. We were a great team . . . but I guess this is where our paths diverge."

Tony's phone system beeped. He noted Pepper's number on the caller ID.

"It's Pepper," he told Stane. "I should take that."

"Tony, please," Stane said. "I'll be out of here in a minute."

Tony nodded and pushed the button that would send the call to voice mail.

Stane put his hand on Tony's shoulder. "We have too much history to part on bad terms," Stane said. "I'd like your blessing."

Tony was about to give it, when suddenly, paralyzing pain shot through his entire body.

Stane stepped back as Tony slumped into a chair. Obadiah placed a device Tony recognized as a sonic Taser down on the table, next to the pizza.

"Easy now," Stane said with a wicked smile. "Try to breathe."

He knelt down and opened Tony's shirt. "You can't mess with progress, Tony," he said. You've created your greatest weapon ever, but you think that means it belongs to *you*. It doesn't—it belongs to the *world*."

Tony tried to speak, but couldn't say anything.

Stane pulled out some tools and began removing the RT heart from the socket in Tony's chest.

"Your 'heart' will be the seed of the next generation of weapons," Stane continued. "They'll help us steer the world back in the right direction—put the balance of power back in the right hands—our hands."

Stane held up the RT device; it cast an eerie glow across his face.

"By the time you die," Stane said, "my prototype will be operational." He wrapped the RT heart in a handkerchief and stuck it in his pocket. He stood, switched off the sonic Taser, and stuck it back in his pocket.

"The sad thing is," Stane finished, "we're *both* the good guys." He turned and left, switching off the lights on his way out.

CHAPTER

17

"**W**hat do you mean he paid to have Tony killed?" Rhodey blared. "Why should Obadiah . . . ? Where is Tony now?"

Pepper tried to keep her voice calm. "I don't know," she said into the receiver. "He's not answering his phone, and Jarvis didn't pick up, either. Will you go to the mansion and check on him? I'm going to look in the labs here."

"Is that safe?" Rhodey asked.

"I've got some government men with me," Pepper replied. "I think we can handle it."

"If Tony's at the mansion, I'll find him," Rhodey assured her.

"Thanks, Rhodey." She signed off, glad that Agent Coulson had brought five other agents with him. They'd need a small army to go against Stane and the resources of Stark Industries.

Her first priority, though—now that she'd convinced Coulson to help her—had to be finding Tony. If he was on campus, the high-tech lab below the ARK Reactor would be the place to start looking. Unfortunately, Stane would know that, too.

A chill ran down Pepper's spine as they headed for the lab. She prayed that she and Rhodey weren't already too late.

Obadiah Stane stepped into the subbasement lab of Stark Industries, below the ARK Reactor. In his hand he held the glowing RT heart he'd stolen. The overhead lights were off; everyone had gone home. Only the dim, red security lights lit his way as he walked purposefully across the room.

The prototype armor—the armor that would make Stark's shareholders even richer—stood in a corner, next to the Sampson cluster machines that had manufactured it and the original armor.

Carefully, Stane opened the new armor's chest plate and locked the stolen heart into place.

The sensors in the faceplate of the helmet glowed to life—twin eyes, burning red in the darkness.

Stane smiled.

Tony gasped for breath as the elevator doors slid open, revealing his workshop. He tried to take a step, but his knees buckled and he fell on his face.

Slowly, painfully, he began crawling across the workshop floor. He could see his goal—encased in Lucite—sitting on the table on the far side of the lab: his old chest piece. Thank heaven Pepper had saved it.

It was less than fifty feet away, but it seemed like miles. Tony's heart pounded in his chest. At any moment, the shrapnel might kill him.

He reached the bench and hoisted himself up, fumbling for the plastic container. His hand brushed against it, knocking the Lucite off the table. The old heart clattered to the floor, but the Lucite didn't break.

Tony seized the container in his hand. The heart's pale glow illuminated his face. The Lucite was much harder than ordinary plastic; Tony wasn't sure he had the strength to break it.

He raised the container as high as he could and smashed it down onto the floor. The Lucite shattered and the glowing chest piece skidded free. Desperately, Tony wrapped his fingers around it.

One of Coulson's agents placed explosives on the hinges of the locked door leading to the sub-basement lab. Pepper's pass code wasn't working for some reason, and none of them wanted to waste time trying to figure out why.

The agent finished inserting the detonators into the explosive and called, "Clear!"

Everyone retreated around the corner of the stairwell and crouched down. The agent pressed the control button and the explosive blew the door off its hinges.

Agent Coulson led the group through the smoking doorway and into the corridor beyond. Pepper noticed the security camera staring down at them from one corner of the ceiling. If Tony was here, would he be watching them? Would Stane?

The huge laboratory ahead was dark, lit only by the blinking lights of the automated machinery, which filled the room almost to overflowing. It had been a long time since Pepper had been down here, and everything looked different—sinister.

"Tony?" she called tentatively. "Obadiah?"

Something moved in the darkness. Pepper jumped. All the agents drew their guns and swung around. Coulson shone a flashlight in that direction.

But it was only a battered suit of armor—apparently the one Tony had used to escape his kidnappers.

"What's that?" Coulson asked.

"New project," Pepper replied. "You shouldn't even be seeing it."

"Looks pretty *old* to me," another of the agents commented.

"I wasn't talking about the armor," Coulson said, "I was talking about the *empty hooks* next to it."

Pepper looked at the hooks, perplexed. Just at that moment, something grabbed one of the agents at the rear of the group and yanked him into the darkness.

Rhodey reeled back and kicked the front door of Tony's mansion off its hinges. Inside, the home was eerily dark and silent; Jarvis didn't greet Rhodey as he entered.

The living room was in shambles. Furniture lay overturned, several lamps had been broken. Incongruously, an untouched, deep-dish pizza lay on the coffee table.

"Tony?" Rhodey called. "Jarvis?"

There was no answer.

"Tony, where are you?"

Rhodey went to the elevator leading to the lab, but it seemed to be locked on the lower floor. He found the stairway and jumped down the steps three at a time. The door to the lab was locked, too, so he kicked it open.

His jaw dropped as he stepped inside. The entire workshop seemed to have been turned into an armory. Electronic components lay everywhere. Rows of helmets, boots, and gauntlets filled the laboratory shelves. Two suits of gleaming armor hung in the middle of the room, suspended by cables that were attached to the ceiling. They looked like the surveillance photos Rhodey had seen of the UAV that attacked the Gulmiran rebels.

"Tony?" he called again.

Tony Stark sat on the far side of the lab, strapped into a high-tech chair. Robotic arms moved around him in an intricate dance, performing surgery on Tony's chest plate.

"Tony, are you all right?" Rhodey asked.

Tony gazed darkly at him. "Obadiah tried to kill me."

"But you're all right?"

The robot arms finished their task and retracted into the ceiling. "I am now," Tony said, standing. He took down the red-and-gold armor and began putting it on.

"What's the plan?" Rhodey asked.

"I'm going after Stane," Tony replied. He finished donning the armor and lowered the helmet over his head.

Rhodey nodded. "I'm right behind you."

Tony nodded back and said, "I'm counting on it." With a sound like a jet engine taking off, his boot rockets fired and he soared out through a ragged hole in the workshop roof.

Rhodey watched for a moment, in awe. Then he remembered the other suit of armor—the silver one. He pulled the helmet off the rack, and admired it.

"Next time, baby," Rhodey said. He raced to the garage on the far side of the lab, picked out the fastest car he could find, and zoomed off, chasing his friend.

Pepper dodged through the lab equipment, trying to keep out of sight. Something terrible had happened, but she couldn't be sure what. The agents—even Coulson—had raced off into the darkened lab, leaving her behind.

Gunfire sounded from somewhere nearby. Bullets burst pipes, spewing steam into the semi-darkness. Pepper moved in the opposite direction, trying to put as much machinery between her and the gunfire as possible.

She plugged her cell phone into her ear and tried to get a signal. Nothing.

Something exploded, and a big piece of metal zipped past. It smashed through several pipes, sending more steam into the air.

An agent stumbled out of the mist toward her. "Agents down! Agents down!" he called into his radio. Spotting Pepper, he added, "Get out of here!"

He pushed her toward the exit, which she could barely make out through the smoke. She ran for it.

Behind her, the lab entryway shattered into a spray of dust and debris, but Pepper didn't dare look back. She ran up the stairway, slowing to catch her breath only when she reached the third landing.

The wall below her shook as something smashed through the door. But the thing was too big for the stairwell; it got stuck in the debris. It was a huge metal suit of armor—much bigger than the one she'd seen hanging in the lab or the one Tony used. It looked like a cross between a man and a tank. Its red eyes glowed in the semidarkness.

Pepper turned and ran as fast as she could. She didn't look back.

When she got outside, she punched Tony's number on her cell phone. Much to her relief, he answered immediately.

"Tony, thank goodness I got you!" she said. "Listen to me—"

"Pepper," Tony replied, "where are you?"

Suddenly, the ground beneath her shook. She toppled sideways, and the earpiece fell from her head. An armored fist blasted through the pavement at her feet. Another fist punched through, widening the hole. The hands peeled the asphalt back like a flimsy candy wrapper.

The armored form of Iron Monger burst up through the crater. Pepper backed away, stumbling over the broken pavement. The iron giant towered over her.

"Look . . . ," Pepper said, backing away.

Iron Monger stepped forward, the ground shaking beneath his boots.

CHAPTER

18

"**P**epper," Tony called, *"duck!"*

Pepper threw herself flat on the ground. Iron Man zoomed over her head, activating the Repulsors in both hands. The blasts hit Iron Monger, and he staggered backward. Iron Man kept coming, smashing his fists into the giant's armored chest.

Iron Monger swiped at Iron Man and grabbed hold of Tony's outstretched gauntlet. Both of them tumbled into the crater Iron Monger had ripped in the pavement.

They crashed through several levels of service tunnels into the subbasement lab. They landed hard, splashing down amid a lake of water and cooling fluid from ruptured pipes. For a moment, steam and debris obscured everything.

As Tony struggled to his feet, the whole building shuddered. Warning lights flashed and a Klaxon horn sounded. The heads-up display in Iron Man's armor relayed a message from the Stark Industries computer systems: ARK REACTOR HOUSING CRACKED. MELTDOWN IMMINENT.

Iron Man walked through the rubble of the lab, but he didn't see Iron Monger—or, for that matter, Obadiah Stane—anywhere. Tony set his systems to scan for his enemy.

"Pepper. . . ," he called over his communications link.

"Tony!" she called back. "Are you okay?"

"I'm fine, but we've got a big problem: The ARK Reactor is melting down. The only way to prevent it is to overload the reactor and discharge the excess power."

"How are you going to do that?" She sounded worried.

"*You're* going to do that," Tony replied.

"Me?"

"Yes. I want you to go to the central panel and close all the low-voltage relays. Then I need you to go to the east wall and close all the eight hundred–amp breakers."

"Tony, I don't know what you're talking about."

Tony kept scanning for Iron Monger, but the

steam, debris, and water were fouling up his imaging systems.

"Pepper," he said, "just turn on all of the little switches. Then turn on all of the big switches."

"Turn them *on*?" she asked. "I thought you wanted me to *close* them. Tony? Do you want me to close them, or turn them on?"

Before he could answer, Iron Monger charged out from under the rubble. Iron Man turned, but the armored giant crashed into his midsection. Tony hurtled backward like a man caught on the horns of a bull.

They smashed through a cement wall and then through the retaining wall that separated the Stark Industries buildings from the nearby highway.

Drivers slammed on their brakes and cars careened out of control as the metal titans crashed down in the middle of the road. An experimental hydrogen-powered bus skidded and slammed into the retaining wall. As Iron Man and Iron Monger stepped apart, the bus's passengers ran for safety.

"Tony," Pepper called, "I need some help here. I closed all the things . . ."

"Go to the TR1 box and hit the red button," he replied.

"Tony, *all* the buttons are red!"

Iron Monger grabbed a station wagon and hefted it over his head. The family inside the car screamed.

"Don't," Tony told him. "This is *our* fight."

"People are always going to die," Iron Monger replied. "It's part of the game."

Tony hit his Repulsors, but nothing happened; probably they'd been damaged in the fight.

"Jarvis, emergency power!" Tony said.

"Sir, you'll drain the—"

"Now!"

Energy surged through the RT in Iron Man's chest plate. A powerful Repulsor burst blasted forth and struck Iron Monger full in the chest, making him stagger. As the giant fell, he heaved the car toward Tony.

Iron Man caught the vehicle, but the weight forced him to his knees. The armor's servos whirred, but their power had been drained by the massive Repulsor blast. Tony's old RT heart didn't have the energy of the new one Stane had stolen.

Iron Man's armor buckled and the station wagon fell on top of him. Iron Monger recovered and thundered toward his victims once more.

"Go, Mom! Go!" a kid in the station wagon cried. The woman inside stomped on the gas and the car took off, dragging Iron Man with it. Sparks flew as Tony's armor scraped across the pavement.

Iron Monger followed, stepping on some cars, batting others out of the way. Drivers that were caught on the roadway stopped and fled from their vehicles.

Tony finally managed to pull himself out from

under the station wagon. He staggered to his feet, his armor smoking. Iron Monger grabbed the front wheel of an abandoned motorcycle and smashed the bike into Iron Man.

Pepper's voice came over the headset. "Tony," she said, "this is *not* looking good."

Iron Man sailed through the air for a hundred yards and smashed into the retaining wall right next to the hydrogen-powered bus. Iron Monger blasted off, his immense bulk hurtling forward like a cannonball.

Tony tried his hand Repulsors again; still no luck. "Jarvis!" he said.

"Working on resolving the problem, sir."

Iron Monger landed on top of Iron Man and pressed one huge boot into his chest.

Tony grunted with the impact and tried to lift the boot off. But saving the station wagon had depleted even more of his power reserves.

"Whoever you are, listen," Tony said. "The ARK Reactor is about to blow up. A lot of people are going to die."

With a creaking, metallic sound, Iron Monger shook his head. "It didn't have to end like this," the giant said. "You were down. You should have stayed down." Slowly, he applied pressure to his boot, crushing Iron Man into the ground.

CHAPTER

Iron Man felt his armor buckling. Iron Monger towered above him, easily twice his size and three times his weight. A roaring sound filled Tony's ears. At first he thought it was the rushing of his own blood.

Then twin headlights blazed in the darkness as a sports car sped right toward them.

Iron Monger spotted the car and turned—too late. The Porsche smashed into the giant's other leg. The leg's armor buckled and Iron Monger careened through the air, his jet boots crippled.

He crashed into a parked bus, bursting its hydrogen tank. Iron Monger struggled to free himself from the wreckage, but his metal fingers set off a spark and . . . WHOOM!

The whole bus went up in a huge fireball.

Tony staggered to his feet. The sports car that had saved him was crushed and mangled, but he still recognized it—and the driver inside.

"Rhodey!" he called, ripping the wreck open so his friend could climb out.

Rhodey grinned at him.

"Did you have to use *my* car?" Tony asked.

Rhodey shrugged. "It's not like you don't have more."

The two of them stared at the bus, now just a mass of flames and molten metal.

"Get this area evacuated," Tony said. "The ARK Reactor is about to melt down." As he spoke, Jarvis finished rerouting his armor's power reserves. Iron Man activated his boots and jetted into the air.

"You could at least say thank you!" Rhodey shouted after him.

"Pepper," Tony called as he flew back toward the reactor, "how's it going?"

"I did everything you told me, but it says 'Circuit not complete,'" she called back.

"I've got to get to the roof," he said. "Sit tight."

Ahead of him, the reactor building glowed more and more brilliantly. Iron Man skidded to a stop on the roof, barely missing an array of satellite dishes.

He called up the building's schematics on his heads-up display and located a thick cable running just beneath the roof's surface. Digging his fingers in, Iron Man ripped up the roofing and exposed the cable.

Using his left gauntlet as a clamp, Tony attached the cable to the row of satellite antennas. The pulsating, greenish light of the overloading reactor shone out through the bank of skylights nearby.

"Pepper," he said, "I'm about to complete the circuit. Once I do, it's going to discharge all of the reactor's power and channel it up through the roof. Get ready to push the Emergency Master Bypass—"

"I've found it!" she called.

"—but, not until I'm off the roof," he finished. "It's going to fry everything up here."

He detached his left gauntlet, leaving the cable clamped in place. The screen on his heads-up display flashed: CIRCUIT COMPLETE.

Tony flipped up his faceplate and wiped the sweat from his eyes. "Pepper," he said, "wait until I fly clear, and then hit the button."

The roof shuddered, and Tony wheeled as Iron Monger landed twenty feet away. Flames still licked around Iron Monger's blackened armor as he lumbered toward Iron Man.

Tony barely managed to get his faceplate down before Iron Monger struck. The giant's huge armored fist smashed into Iron Man's chest.

Iron Man skidded back across the rooftop and tumbled to his feet. He blasted off, flying straight for his enemy. Schematics of Iron Monger armor appeared on Tony's heads-up display, showing the probable location of the giant's hydraulic control systems.

Iron Man reached for the controls with his remaining gauntlet, but Iron Monger spun and caught him in a massive bear hug. Tony gasped as his armor began to crack under the pressure. Inside his helmet, the heads-up display crystals splintered and went dark.

"Jarvis," Tony gasped. "Deploy counter measures!"

Instantly compartments on the armor flipped open and a thousand particles of chaff exploded, filling the air with smoke, flame, and bits of metal.

Surprised, Iron Monger lost his grip and Tony rocketed free. He landed behind his foe and ripped Iron Monger's hydraulics loose.

Iron Monger staggered, and Iron Man punched him. The giant fell back, flailing desperately. His metal fingers latched onto Iron Man's helmet. He whirled, tossing Iron Man like a doll.

Iron Man bounced to a halt atop the bank of skylights above the ARK Reactor core. Tony gasped as the evening breeze ruffled his hair. Iron Monger had ripped off his helmet!

The giant laughed as he crushed the depowered helmet like a tin can.

Iron Man staggered to his feet, standing atop the skylights. He and Iron Monger faced each other. Iron Monger lumbered forward, and Tony realized, for the first time, that the giant's armor had built-in machine guns.

Tony jumped aside as Iron Monger sprayed the roof with bullets. The huge glass skylights shattered beneath Iron Man, but without his helmet controls, he couldn't fire his jets.

He caught onto the side of the roof at the last instant. He heard a gasp below him and, glancing down, saw Pepper standing near the reactor core. As Tony pulled himself back onto the roof, Iron Monger kept shooting.

Iron Man's armor stopped a few glancing blows, but Tony knew that without his helmet, sooner or later his luck would run out.

"Pepper!" he shouted down through the sky-lights. "Hit the button!"

"You said not to!" she shouted back.

"Just do it!" Tony cried as another bullet dented his armor.

"But you're not off the roof!"

"Pepper, we have no choice! We have to stop him! Do it now!"

CHAPTER

Pepper hit the button and dived for cover under the nearby consoles.

A pulse of electromagnetic energy flashed upward along the reactor housing and through the cable Tony had rigged up. The energy arced across the satellite dishes, vaporizing the roof between them.

The pulse spread outward, killing the power of everything it touched. The lab went dark, then the building, then the rest of the Stark Industries compound. And, on the roof of the ARK Reactor, the power to both suits of armor died as well.

Iron Monger and Iron Man stopped dead in their tracks, frozen like statues.

More ARK energy burst forth. The roof shuddered and began to buckle and sag. Tony glanced down at his chest. His RT heart was dark and cold. He knew he didn't have much time.

Iron Monger's armor, which was closest to the section of roof that had been vaporized, toppled over. Only by luck did its depowered fingers catch the edge of the roof as it slid down the slope.

Tony's heart pounded in his chest. Sweat poured down his head. Using every bit of strength he possessed, he forced his armor to move, reaching out to save his enemy.

"Take my hand!" he called to Iron Monger.

But Tony suddenly realized that his foe wasn't trying to escape from the crippled giant's armor; he was trying to manually winch open the his rocket launcher.

But doing so loosened Iron Monger's grip on the sagging roof. With a sudden jolt, the giant began to slide again.

"Noooo . . . !" Iron Monger called as he plunged over the ledge and into the reactor core. With a roof-shaking hiss, the white-hot plasma swallowed him and Iron Monger vanished forever.

Tony shook his head. Now he would never know who had been inside that armor. He closed his eyes and waited on the roof, trying to steady himself. But with Iron Monger gone, the roof didn't sag any farther. Ten minutes later, a pair of flashlights played across the surface of Iron Man's lifeless armor.

Tony opened his eyes and saw Rhodey and Pepper running toward him.

They pulled him away from the precipice and off the roof. Eventually, Jarvis—whose mainframe had been far enough away to avoid the electro-magnetic pulse—managed to restore the armor's power.

Tony looked at the RT heart in his chest. It glowed faintly. Tony breathed a sigh of relief. He'd had a very close call, but Iron Man would live to fight another day.

Days later, Tony and Pepper walked along the hallway of Stark Industries. Pepper, who was carrying a stack of newspapers and documents, shoved a typewritten paper into his hands.

"Here's your alibi," she said to him. "You were on your yacht, *Avalon*, during the whole incident. I've got port papers that put you there all night and sworn statements from fifty of your guests."

"Maybe it was just the two of us," Tony suggested. "On the yacht, I mean."

"Focus, please," she said.

He scooped up a newspaper from the stack she was carrying and read the headline: WHO IS IRON MAN?

Tony shook his head. Already the battle seemed like a half-remembered dream. His people had never found the Iron Monger armor; apparently, the ARK Reactor had vaporized it. Obadiah Stane hadn't turned up, either. Tony could only assume he'd gone into hiding.

"Iron Man . . . ," Tony mused. "Not a technically accurate name, since the armor is mostly carbon-fiber and ceramic . . . But I like the ring of it. 'Iron Man.'"

He stopped suddenly as he and Pepper turned the corner. She looked at him questioningly. He gazed into her eyes.

"You know that night at the concert hall?" he said. "Do you ever think about it?"

Pepper smiled slightly and then turned away. "I don't know what you're talking about." She reached out and fixed his unruly tie. "Will that be all, Mr. Stark?"

He straightened up. "That will be all, Ms. Potts."

As he walked away, Tony Stark smiled.

For Iron Man, this was only the beginning.